Children and dogs are as necessary to the welfare of the country as Wall Street and the railroads.

> —*Harry S. Truman*
> *(He didn't read the book.)*

This book is more about rolling rocks than it is about rocking rolls.

> —*Jenny Ego*
> *(She is a fictitious character in the book.)*

This book absolutely rocks! Well, if you ask me, when you don't want a book to ever end and you grow fond of all its characters, even the "bad guys," THAT'S definitely a pretty darn good book you're holding in your hand, and that's what *The English Setter Dance* is to me: a good, compelling book like I have not read in ages. So my big thanks go to the author. This book was a gift and not because I was given a copy as a present (indeed I bought it myself) but a gift for my spirits. Sure, you've got to love rock music (like I do) and dogs (I'm even "owned" by an English Setter myself) but you'll best enjoy reading it if you are wont to endlessly wonder about life and its purpose.

> —*Elena Scarani*
> *(She actually read the book and posted this on Amazon.com)*

THE ENGLISH SETTERS SÉANCE

A Tale of Rock Music and Dogs

THE ENGLISH SETTER DANCE

ISBN-10:   0-9840773-4-0
ISBN-13:   978-0-9840773-4-2

Published by:
Two Peas Publishing
Columbia, TN U.S.A.

The cover photo of The English Setter Dance was taken by Rock 'n' Roll Randy. Thanks Randy! The band members are:
Preston Ely
Domenic Marcantonio
Holly Trasti
Kevin Kimmes
They are members of Beach Patrol and Holly and the Non-Italians.

Please buy their albums:
Beach Patrol: *It's Only Greener 'Till You Get There* and *Riding Dinosaurs*
Holly and the Non-Italians: *self-titled*
Their music is local rock music—where rock music always exists.

The photo of Lola on the back cover is by Julie Molzahn.
Peter Honsberger first put the halo on her.

Bill Golembeski

COLUMBIA, TENNESSEE

In loving memory of Ivy, Leslie, and Ruby:
Setters all and all good girls.

And Dad.

"Dogs got more sense than to sleep in the rain
But they can't play rock and roll."
—Michael Chapman

THE PRE-RAMBLE

I have come to the conclusion that there are no rock 'n' roll bands in Hell. Don't ask me how I know this. It's only an idea.

The same is true for dogs. They just don't exist in Hell.

Once when I was drinking a cup of tea at a cafeteria table in London's big war museum, an old man in an overcoat with medals pinned to the pocket asked me if Hell had been specifically designed for humans or if we had to share its torments with alien beings from other planets. The old man said he had fought in the trench warfare in World War I and he had killed Germans. He said he had bayoneted a wounded man through the chest. The German, he said, bled so quietly that he couldn't hear the blood.

Blood should be heard, so he bayoneted him again.

He showed me the medals and then said he was certain that he was going to Hell because he had killed the wounded German soldier who had bled in such deafening silence. He hated the idea of weird alien creatures from other planets being with him in Hell because they might not understand the fear that had caused him to bayonet a wounded man in a filthy, war-pocked trench in France.

So the old soldier asked me if I thought Hell was reserved

for evil humans, not aliens. I laughed because I thought he was joking.

He was not.

So I stopped laughing.

I told him that I really didn't know anything about aliens or Hell. He was disappointed. I apologized several times. The old man nodded his head and fell silent, as if he were searching for words. I looked at his medals and expected him to say something profound, but then he simply recovered himself and thanked me.

He thanked me even though I had been unable to tell him anything about aliens and Hell.

I still think—even after all these years—it was quite a decent thing for him to do.

He thanked me even though I had not answered his question, and I think that question meant a lot to him.

That same old man then informed me that he thought there were no dogs in Hell.

He said a stray dog had somehow wandered into the trenches of his battlefield. The dog made him smile, even in the middle of war. When he looked into the sad canine eyes, his feet were not as wet, his hands were not as bloody, his guilt was less severe; and he knew his night would not be riddled with dreams of detonations and the suffocating smoke of death.

He sipped his tea slowly as he spoke. I sipped my tea as well. Such sad dog eyes, he said, could never exist in Hell.

That's why I know there are no dogs in Hell.

I talked with a man who had killed another man. The two of us sat in a big war museum in London, and he told me a dying man's blood should be heard.

Of course, he didn't know anything about rock 'n' roll bands. He never mentioned anything about *Hamlet*. The sad old guy just said he knew there were no dogs in Hell, although not once did he ever discuss Heaven.

As I said, it's only an idea.

It's just a rumor.

But there's always a little truth in rumor—even if that truth is just a bit of a rambling story.

LOVE AT FIRST SIGHT

In those days, my thoughts were always about women.

So that's what I was doing when the bright sunrise struck my unfocused eyes that morning. I was thinking about women. I opened my eyes for a moment and then quickly closed them in the glare of the sun's rays. And I thought about women again. Suddenly, I felt the kiss of warm lips with gentle breath.

Was this a dream?

I opened my sleepy eyes again and tried to focus in the bright June morning light. Soft brown eyes filled my view. They were doe-like, delicately beautiful.

A tongue brushed across my mouth, then my nose. I felt the tickle of love, the paintbrush of affection, the first of countless promised kisses. A second kiss, and my mouth felt wet. I laughed with pleasure.

I thought about Molly, a girl I had met the previous night. She had been on my mind ever since. Then my thoughts wandered to other women. I remembered Leslie's dark eyes, Ivy's wavy hair, and Ruby with her wet feet. Ruby still in her graduation dress. Ruby with her bow undone.

I smiled. I was still half asleep. I met each of those girls in the early morning of my high school graduation party.

LOVE AT FIRST SIGHT

They were drunk and giddy. And that was my last look at high school: three tipsy girls who said they liked rock music.

I smiled again.

I always smiled when I thought about women.

"Lola!" a commanding voice chided from somewhere in the sunlight.

My eyes tried to focus. Then they blurred again with more wet lips and wet kisses.

"Lola!" the voice was stern. "Lola! Get off him right now!"

I raised my hands and pushed a hairy bony body away from me. Its elbows worked like little piston levers, trying to spring closer to me, trying to kiss me again.

"Lola! Down girl! Get off! Right now!"

The hairy body was pulled from me as my vision finally crystallized on the most beautiful dog I had ever seen.

Lola's face was white except for a raven mask that covered one eye. A brown patch of fur shaped like a lightning bolt slashed across her cheek. A brown spot was dabbed over her other eye, adding a little deeper mystery to the Yin and Yang of her black-and-white setter face. Her dog feet tap-danced like Gene Kelly on the floor of the wood cabin, as if she were hoping for another chance to lick, to smell, and to love another human.

Richard, whom I had met the previous night, tugged at the dog's collar and apologized.

"Sorry," he said. "She's an English setter. She just likes humans a lot. That's the way setters are. They're loving dogs."

"Lola," I said. "I like the name."

6

I looked at that setter face again.

"That's a great name for a dog."

"Yeah, it's from a Kinks song. You know, 'Lola.' The song about this guy who's dancing with a girl but it turns out to be a man."

He paused.

"Hey! Watch this!" Richard picked up his guitar and strummed a few chords. I recognized the song from the radio. It had been popular for a while.

Sometime while Richard was singing, Molly entered the room. I didn't notice at first because I was too busy being licked by a dog.

Molly sang the high harmony of the chorus. God! She could sing.

Richard continued to strum the rhythm of the song while Lola's tail wagged rapidly with the melody. Lola raised her front paws off the floor and, with awkward balance, took three quick steps forward. Then she swung those front paws and bent her hind legs back and forth in a decent imitation of one of the back-drop go-go singers who filled the space behind Chubby Checker as he twisted and sang on American Bandstand. It was quite the show.

Finally, on the final strum of the guitar, Lola fell back on all four paws and crinkled her upper lip, grinning her dog smile at me and baring her teeth.

"Good girl!" Molly clapped her hands in approval.

Lola trotted to Richard, and he tickled her ears.

"Yes," he said. "Good girl. You're a very good girl."

He looked at me.

"She only dances to that one song. We didn't even have to teach her. She just likes the song a lot, so we named our band after her."

"Lola?" I asked.

Richard laughed.

"No, we're The English Setter Dance. That's the group's name. You know, like Buffalo Springfield. You've heard of them. Or Jethro Tull, Mott the Hoople, Fairport Convention.

"They're all great bands with great names. Like Yes and King Crimson."

I have to be honest. I liked the name the very first time I heard it. I still like it. Mind you, this was a time before the advent of punk rock and hard-core bands, who sought monosyllabic words of pestilential epidemics for their monikers rather than the vaguely pretty and imaginative names of this era. Even after all these years and slogging through such band names as Parasites, Inhalants, Leper Colony, The Sewer Slugs, and Dog Piss, I have to confess to a heartfelt fondness for The English Setter Dance. It's a good name for a rock band.

"I really like the name," I said.

Lola grinned at me, crinkled her lip, and sneezed.

Apparently, she liked the name too.

I returned her smile. Then she even jumped in my lap and demanded an ear tickle. She licked my hand and refused to allow me to stop giving her the attention and affection she desired.

Setters are like that.

It was love at first sight, indeed.

THE REVOLUTION

I had only met Richard, Molly, and Lola—their dancing setter—the previous night at my uncle's cabin located in the woods of Point Beach State Forest. In Wisconsin, we have this mythical wonderland called Up North. No one really knows where this vacation paradise is located, but we know it when we finally find Up North. We just *know* when we are there. And, somehow, we all feel better when we get there.

At the same time, the early 1970s, there was a similar mythical destination that we, the youth of America, called The Revolution. That's how I caught up with Richard, Molly, Lola, and the musical wind called The English Setter Dance. Honest! I was simply looking for The Revolution.

I had hitchhiked the thirty miles from Green Bay so that I could retreat, at least for a while, to the simplicity of my uncle's cabin. Strangers in big automobiles passed me by without so much as a second glance as I stood, thumb outstretched, hoping for a ride.

All sorts of drivers, their eyes starched and gazing forward, refused to stop.

They were obviously not part of The Revolution.

They were part of The System.

THE REVOLUTION

Finally, a car did stop, and the driver turned out to be my cousin Tommy, in his old Dodge Dart Swinger.

Tommy had a beard and attended the Big-Ten ultra-radical University of Wisconsin in Madison.

I think he studied the philosophy of life.

People did that sort of thing in 1974.

I recognized Tommy's Dodge because the passenger door was Rustoleum red, although the rest of the car was yellow.

He saw me and pulled over.

Yes, my cousin Tommy was a part of The Revolution; he was listening to an eight-track tape called *Alpha Centauri* by a weird German space band called Tangerine Dream. One song on that tape was nearly twenty minutes long.

As the miles on the odometer clicked by, we talked about music and politics—two mandatory topics for all card-carrying members of The Revolution. We both hoped The Beatles and Crosby, Stills, Nash, and Young would record more albums. For those who don't know, The Beatles and CSN&Y were two bands who sang quite a bit about topics of The Revolution, such as peace, love, and brotherhood.

Unfortunately, both bands split because their members couldn't stand each other.

That was a shame.

Their music was really good.

Tommy offered to give me a lift to a bar called The Sled Shed, the owner of which held the key to my uncle's cabin. It was dusk, and we could already hear music playing as we left the Dodge outside The Shed.

THE ENGLISH SETTER DANCE

Inside, a chalkboard over the bar read:

Playing Tonight:
ROCK MUSIC
The Push-Snowblowers
No Cover!!

The band wasn't very loud. I could understand the lyrics to their songs. But I thought their name was a bit odd. If they ever made it big and cut a great album, most people outside of Wisconsin's midwest snow-belt would not get the name. Truth be told, I shouldn't have worried. Unfortunately for their own future, the band played a variety of rock 'n' roll called progressive rock, which was championed by bands like Yes, King Crimson, Pink Floyd, Genesis, and, to some degree, Led Zeppelin. It was a subculture of a sound that produced music with nasty time signatures, great keyboard work, lavish epic-length songs, quasi-intellectual lyrics, and a general ambience that precluded dancing and excessive drinking while listening.

Progressive rock demanded the audience be attentive, patient, and somewhat intelligent. Therefore, The Snowblowers never really had to worry about being popular and selling lots of records.

They did try hard, though.

The lead singer was dressed in a magician's outfit and, after a long keyboard solo, he sang some lyrics explaining that God kept a long record of our choices we make every day on a test sheet. When we die, he sang, the test sheet is fed into a big correcting machine in Heaven. Apparently, sixty percent of correct choices gets you a ticket to Heaven.

It wasn't exactly "Love Me Do," but I liked the melody, and it reminded me of a short story I read in high school. When it was over, I applauded.

But I was the only one.

One guy yawned, two girls got up to leave, and someone at the bar tried to pour beer from a pitcher into his glass. He was too drunk, so the beer spilled all over the floor.

I don't think he noticed the mess, though, because he kept pouring more beer.

I stayed for another song. It was about the aliens who crashed at Roswell, New Mexico, in the 1940s while listening to Bachman-Turner Overdrive at the moment of impact. The Snowblowers' lead singer, who was still dressed as a magician, explained that aliens listening to Bachman-Turner Overdrive when they crashed in 1947 proved that time travel was, indeed, possible; and apparently the United States generals at the base didn't want their soldiers who had to go to war to know it. So there was a big cover-up about the alien crash.

I guess the song was some sort of antiwar statement. Why would soldiers go into battle if the outcome was pre-destined by the Fates, Nostradamus, or Wall Street?

It was a long song, but the band managed to include a little bit of BTO's big hit single, "You Ain't Seen Nothing Yet," into the text of the tune. When The Snowblowers hit BTO's familiar chords, three girls jumped up and began to dance and somebody screamed, "Boogie!" But that catchy part only lasted for a minute or two and then the keyboard player wandered off on another solo in some weird time signature.

The girls sat down, and everyone else in the bar looked disappointed. The drunken guy at the bar just continued to try to pour beer into his glass.

When the band took a break, I found The Shed's owner, who held the key to my uncle's cabin. He told me to come back again, and then added: "Don't worry." He motioned at the stage. "They aren't coming back."

I nodded.

I thought it was the right thing to do.

"Yeah," he said. "We've got two bands Saturday night. They'll be better than those Snowblowers."

I nodded again.

He ran an index finger down the paper schedule on the wall.

"Let's see," he said. "Tomorrow, we've got a band. Yeah. The band is called The Lactose Tolerant."

He smiled.

"The names these days. What is a Lactose Tolerant? I thought it has something to do with milk. Drinking it or something. Give me Iron Butterfly any day, you know? Or The Beatles. Where are The Beatles? The Stones. You know. Those are names."

He shook his head.

"Then we've got two bands on Saturday. One's called All You Can Eat and Drink and the other band is The English Setter Dance. Some guy from the band came here a few days ago and said they'll play for free."

He grinned.

"Sure, free music. What do I have to lose? They have to be better than whatever was on tonight. I said they could open the show. I'll charge a buck for the other group."

Of course, at the time I had not yet become acquainted with Richard, Molly, and their dancing setter, but I nodded in agreement.

"Yeah. I'll be there," I said. "They sound great. Saturday, right?"

He nodded.

"Here's your key," he said, holding it up, but not extending it to me.

"Thanks," I replied.

"Your uncle's a good guy."

"Yeah. Well, he said I could use his cabin. I want to live there for a little while. I want to get away from everybody. I just want to live by myself. I just want to figure out what I want to do."

He handed me the key.

"Well," he said, "Good luck."

I laughed.

"I'll need it."

I didn't realize at the time his parting comment, "good luck," was probably the greatest phrase in the English language. Those two simple words cast dice at kind gods for parted seas. I just took the key and walked out of his bar. "Good luck" was all he said, but to this day I truly believe he meant it. That was a great thing to say to me.

It's a great thing to say to anyone.

When I departed The Shed, I found the lead singer of The Push-Snowblowers standing outside and leaning on a car. He was smoking a cigarette. He was still dressed in a magician's costume.

"I liked your band."

"Thanks. It's tough. We play our own stuff."

"I liked that Roswell song," I said.

"That's our antiwar song. People just don't get that one."

" I never wanted to go to Vietnam," I explained. "Did you write it?"

"No. The Clap wrote it. We get all the lyrics from Jenny. She sends the words to us, but The Clap wrote it."

"The Clap?" I asked.

"Yeah. He's our guitarist. We call him The Clap. He's really great. He can play anything." His smile faded. "It's just too bad he's leaving the band."

"He's leaving?"

"Yeah. This is his last gig."

"Why?" I asked.

"It's just one of those things."

"Musical differences?" I asked.

"No. He wrote many of the songs."

"Did he find Jesus?" I inquired. That frequently happened to musicians back then.

"I doubt it," he said, and then he laughed. "The Clap never mentioned anything about that sort of thing."

Another idea occurred to me.

"There must have been a girl. Some woman? You must have slept with his girl or something."

"No," he said. "Nothing like that. He just left the band."

"Why?" I persisted.

"Well, we've changed our name," he admitted finally. "We've changed the name of the band."

"So?" I didn't understand.

"Now we're called The Lactose Tolerant."

"Wait a minute," I said, recalling The Shed's upcoming shows. "You're playing here tomorrow."

The singer winced and waved his hands in the air. "Don't say that too loud. That's what we do. This progressive rock's not very popular. We love it, but nobody else does. We change our name all the time to get gigs."

"And that works?"

"It gets us a few shows. Nobody books us twice. They hate our music. That's all right. We just play what we like."

"But your guitarist left."

"Yeah." He smiled. "You don't play guitar, do you?"

"I wish," I said.

"The Clap's going to be tough to replace."

"So, remind me why he left?"

"The name."

"The Lactose Tolerant?"

"Yeah," he said. "The Clap doesn't like milk."

"Milk?"

"He's a great guitarist, but he's a really intense guy. He just couldn't deal with the new name. You know. Milk and lactose. That's a shame because after that we're playing as All You Can Eat and Drink. He wouldn't mind that name."

"Unless he's on a diet," I said.

"Yeah. Good point. I'll have to talk to Jenny about that. I'd like to get him back in the band."

"Jenny, your lyricist?"

"Jenny Ego. Yeah, she's our poet. Every band has a poet. She doesn't play any instrument or anything. She just writes the lyrics and thinks up names for us. King Crimson, Elton John, Procol Harum: they all have poets."

"So she wrote that stuff about the Roswell aliens and Bachman-Turner Overdrive?"

"Sure," he said. Then he pulled an envelope from his pocket. "These are brand new."

I read the title: "We Came in Peace for All Mankind."

Inside, there were several pages of lyrics about dogs and aliens and space travel.

"This is really long," I said. "This song is going to go on forever."

"It's an epic. It lasts thirty-five minutes. We might make it longer. Now all I have to do is fit these words into the music."

"And people will like that? That's a long time to listen to one song."

"We don't worry about that. We just do what we like." He winked at me.

"Then," he said, "then we change our name."

As I listened to the singer's words, my cousin Tommy surfaced in my thoughts. He was just like this guy and his band. He didn't care about what other people wanted. He majored in life at college, even though his dad wanted him to be an accountant.

This was all part of The Revolution.

Likewise, I decided that I wanted to do what I really desired for once in my life.

I wanted to listen to that long song about dogs and aliens and space travel.

I wanted to be part of The Revolution.

THE REVOLUTION (AGAIN)

So The Lactose Tolerant was once The Push-Snowblowers, who, in turn, would become All You Can Eat and Drink. Nothing is what you expect, or even want it to be—even in The Revolution.

Nothing stays the same.

For example, I expected my uncle's cabin to be empty.

It wasn't.

That was the night I found Richard where he wasn't supposed to be, silhouetted in the candlelight, larger than life, and, of course, practicing his guitar.

That's exactly how I like to remember Richard Lamm: playing his guitar in the dim light of that candle.

Of course, I was shocked to find that my place of solitude was already inhabited.

Richard just continued to play when I walked in the door.

He should have asked, "Who's there?" like Bernardo at the beginning of *Hamlet*. But Richard just continued to play his guitar until he finished his song.

"You own this place?" he asked, nonchalantly.

"Well, yeah," I said. "My uncle owns it. But you're not

supposed to be here."

Richard began to strum his guitar again.

"It's all right," he said. "Don't get upset. We're just a band. We need a place to hang out and get it together. No one is ever here. We just rehearse. You know. We're going to play out when we're ready. It's no big deal."

But it was a big deal because at that moment I had found my Revolution. The exit door to my PG-cinema life had opened, and I was rushing headlong through that door to the world of R-rated films. It was simply more exciting to be cool than to make a big deal of the whole thing.

"Sure," I said. "You can practice here."

"My uncle," I started, and then corrected myself. "I don't mind if you guys are here."

If I had doubts about my new membership in The Revolution, they went the way of all magic dragons as another uninvited guest, a rather beautiful girl, slowly walked into the dim candlelight of the room. Richard continued to play and Molly brushed her dark hair away from her eyes.

"What's wrong?" she asked, looking from Richard to me. As far as I was concerned, nothing was wrong. Suddenly everything was perfect. But Richard spoke first.

"Aw, nothing," he said. "This is the guy who owns the place. But I think he's cool."

Yes. I was certainly trying to be cool. Of course I was trying to be cool.

And at that instant, I pledged allegiance to their Revolution.

And I had yet to meet their wonderful English setter named Lola.

A HISTORICAL NOTE:

By the early 1970s, when this story takes place, the youth of America had a bone to pick with the status quo-entrenched silent majority system in America. This status quo America had, of course, been sending its youth culture to fight the war in Vietnam for some time; and some of that youth culture had returned in the coffins of an undeclared war. I knew people who had died. In all fairness, I think that The Revolution had a reason to gripe.

Even from my young protracted vantage point of nightly TV dinners and TV tables and TV news reports, Vietnam just looked like a real mess, an awful bloody mess. One time, my family watched one man shoot another man, who had his hands tied behind his back, right in the head. We all watched a cataract of blood spout from the man's right temple. My mother was obviously upset at the news report. After all, we were eating dinner. But of more importance, she had three sons approaching draft age; she had three sons who might have to get involved in the Vietnam mess.

She walked defiantly to the TV and changed the channel. To her horror, the very same war footage was being shown. We all watched, again, as one man shot the other man with his hands tied behind his back, right in the head.

My mother changed to a third channel, and sure enough, there was the same man shooting the other same man with his same hands tied behind his back, right in the very same head. Thank goodness this occurred before the advent of cable TV. Thank goodness we only had three channels. With the modern technology of today, there is no telling how many times that man with his hands tied behind his back might have to die.

My dad, who seldom spoke to any of us as he quietly read his newspaper at the dinner table, put his paper down for a moment and demanded to know the reason for my mother's channel changing. There, on the front page of his paper, in living and dying black and white, was the still photo of the man shooting the other man with his hands tied behind his back, right in the head.

I stared at the picture until my father, sensing he might have to converse with the rest of his family during dinner, raised the paper and blocked his eyes from our view. He never said another word about it. Neither did my mother, who had about the same odds of avoiding that grim portrait of the Vietnam War as did the man with his hands tied behind his back and a gun to his head had of avoiding that bullet through his brain.

On the back page of my father's paper was a Charlie Brown Peanuts cartoon. I quickly read the four panels. Lucy told Charlie Brown she would hold a football for him while he kicked a field goal. Charlie Brown, as always, was gullible and believed her promise. He trusted her. As he approached the ball, she lifted it into the air. Charlie Brown sincerely tried to kick the ball but missed and landed flat on his back.

I laughed and ate the cherry cobbler in the top left corner of my TV dinner tray.

Yes, looking back on that Vietnam mess, I think the youth culture had a reason to gripe.

# # #

That first night with Richard and Molly was a world away from High School, USA. Richard talked about rock music like it was the touch of at least one deity. It is perhaps difficult for modern youth to understand, but in 1974 the avid music listener went without meals to seek the manna of wisdom from the big bands of the day like Pink Floyd, The Kinks, Led Zeppelin, The Moody Blues, or Canada's The Guess Who—our midwestern favorite who graced us with frequent concerts.

I remember the look in Richard's eyes as he recited the words from that other interrogatory band The Who, one of his favorite groups.

"Leave," he insisted. "The Who sang about it. Christ said it. It's all in the Bible." Then I heard his mantra.

"Just leave the shrine.

"Leave the temple.

"It's as simple as that.

THE REVOLUTION (AGAIN)

"Society wants you to stay stupid and locked up in their Tower of Babel.

"Leave.

"Let down your hair, Rapunzel.

" 'Walk away Renee.'

"That's all there is to it."

I agreed with Richard that night. It's always easy to agree with someone who's right. I just hoped that when my time came to leave the temple—when my time came to let down my hair and to walk away—I would have the strength to leave. I have to admit, though, at the time I had no idea how difficult it is to walk away. I had no idea how difficult it is to leave the temple.

The temple, as I have sadly come to realize, doesn't have many doors opening from the inside of its marble walls.

That's just the way it is.

That's the way it has always been.

I asked Richard about the song he was playing when I found him in the cabin. It had a great melody.

"That," he said, "was the very first song I ever wrote. It's called 'Hold Me Tight on This Rock 'n' Roll Night.' I wrote it when I was fifteen. It's about a guy and a girl who fall in love, and they hold each other for the first real time on a cold night in the fall. It's really cold. But they just stand there at the end of their date. They don't want to leave. So they just stand there, breathing frost into the cold night air.

"It doesn't make any sense for them to stay. Their hands are freezing, but they just stand there. They have to hold each other, even when their hands ache. They're in love, so they stand there freezing.

"Tomorrow doesn't count. It's too far away. It's like being in Paris when you're supposed to be in New York.

"That's part of rock music.

"That's what the song is about, being somewhere and not being somewhere else you're supposed to be and not really caring about anything.

"You know what I mean?"

He sang a few words from his song:

This moment is all we've got,
So praise all gods and thanks a lot.

He smiled.

"That's my favorite chorus. It was just luck. Yeah, good luck.

"The song was about only having a moment, and knowing it, so the moment becomes really important. It's kind of a silly song. But it's about rock 'n' roll and being young and being in love.

"Those things don't make much sense: love and being young and rock music. They're crazy sometimes. They even kill people. But they sure make you feel good.

"So you stand there with your hands freezing and aching.

"That's what the song is all about. You know. Praise all gods and thanks a lot. Thanks for the moment. Thanks for the music. Thanks for being young."

That was the very first Richard Lamm music I ever heard.

I liked the song. I liked his explanation. I still sing the words to his chorus. They mean a lot to me, even after all

THE REVOLUTION (AGAIN)

these years.

Music is strong stuff.

Later in life, I talked with my cousin Tommy about his old Tangerine Dream records and his yellow Dodge Dart with the Rustoleum red door. He said that he gave all those records away when he left college, and he bought a Chrysler New Yorker when he took a job in middle management with Ray-O-Vac, a big battery company.

He shaved his beard and wore a suit everyday to work because his battery company told him to wear one.

I don't think he is part of The Revolution any more.

That's a shame, just like all those records The Beatles and Crosby, Stills, Nash, and Young never made.

TWO NECESSARY
HIGH SCHOOL FLASHBACKS

I remember as I walked across the stage in June of 1974 to shake someone's hand and receive my diploma, that I was certain that I had only learned two things during my years in high school. At that moment, I figured I knew the price of an apple, and I knew that Buzz Hogey could never make it as a big-time drug dealer.

I had learned the cost of an apple while watching the smart people in my algebra infinity class solve math problems. There was an incomprehensible word problem in the math book about the cost of apples. Of course, there was always an incomprehensible word problem in the math book. As I recall, there were several letters of the alphabet multiplied by several other letters of the alphabet. We called this arrangement of characters "math sex" in an effort to make it more interesting. Frankly, it was still just algebra to me.

This particular word problem stumped even the really acute math minds. Of course, there was always one guy who knew the answer.

His name was Mark Leistermier.

TWO NECESSARY HIGH SCHOOL FLASHBACKS

He always knew all the answers.

The kid was a math genius.

"Sixty-seven cents," he said.

He didn't even have to use a calculator, which barely existed at the time anyway.

Mark was branded a "math giant." Teachers and students would whisper as he walked through the halls of the school. They whispered, "The boy is a math genius. He's going places."

Cheerleaders considered dating him. Even the custodians asked him to polish up their taxes. That was amazing because, let's face it, the custodians know everything. They even know more than the school secretaries, and that's quite a bit.

Mark had it made, being, as he was, a "math giant." Only English ever made him sweat.

Miss Meyer, an English teacher, once assigned everyone the task of writing a short story. She was a tough teacher. She read our essays. Mark broke out in a fit of perspiration that would have given the shower room a run for its money, although he did figure out how to survive the experience.

He did what we all did: he found someone else to do the work for him.

Mark talked his lab partner, a girl who was our self-proclaimed class valedictorian, into giving him a story. She loved writing stories. She would later write the lyrics to The Push-Snowblowers' song about Roswell aliens and Bachman-Turner Overdrive. Jenny Ego was the *nom de plume* of our very own Jennifer Rachelle Egolenski-short story writer *par excellence* and lab partner to a "math giant."

Jenny wrote a story and gave it to Mark Leistermier, who knew all about math but didn't have a creative bone in his body. According to Jenny's story, everything each of us does, every decision made during each day, is indelibly marked on a lifetime scantron sheet in Heaven. (This, of course, made sense because it was very similar to the scantron sheets we filled out every day in school.) The scantron sheet, when we die, is fed into God's big grading machine. Our entrance into the Heavenly Kingdom of Everlasting Paradise is contingent upon scoring sixty percent on life's multiple choice test. Sixty percent was the magic number, and that was that. The conflict in the story involved a number of recently departed souls who desperately wanted to argue with God about their answers, which had been marked INCORRECT by God's scantron machine.

The unhappy souls were angry, and they yelled at God, but–let's face it–multiple choice scantron tests make God's grading work a snap. And sixty percent is sixty percent. That's what was needed. That was that.

But not everyone was unhappy in Jenny's story. Abe Lincoln, for example, scored a ninety-seven. That was really good.

Vince Lombardi, the famous coach of The Green Bay Packers and the patron saint of every Wisconsinite who ever tossed the pigskin in a backyard scrimmage, earned a ninety-two. His decision to go for the touchdown with fourth and inches in the

TW© NE©ESSARY HI©H S©H©©L FLASHBA©KS

Ice Bowl was a biggie.

And Flipper was there. Flipper, or at least the dolphin who played the part in the first six episodes, swam in a really big tank of water. The dolphin's real name was Ernie, and he had struggled for years on the Sea World Circuit. Ernie had finally made the big-time as the star of everyone's favorite dolphin adventure series. Unfortunately, after all that difficult work and swimming in the first few shows, Ernie took a vacation and was tragically caught in a tuna net and subsequently drowned. Flipper (*nee* Ernie) earned a perfect score.

That was not all that surprising, though.

Dolphins are wonderful creatures.

Jack Ruby, the man who shot Lee Harvey Oswald, who shot President John F. Kennedy, was also there. He argued about his low scantron score, and he begged God for some extra-credit. Meanwhile, Lee Harvey flunked with a thirty-two.

JFK squeaked by with a sixty-one.

Jenny made Mark Leistermier take her to the prom as payment for writing the story for him. She picked out Mark's tuxedo. The tux she chose was robin's egg blue.

Mark also had to wear a shirt with wavy frills down the front. Everyone wore wavy frills in those days, so Jenny's choice wasn't a big deal.

At the time, I did not know Jenny Egolenski's future would include rock 'n' roll music. I liked her valedictory speech, and I heard she planned to continue working at a local grocery store where she was a bit of a local hero because she had been instrumental in putting snow tires on all the shopping carts. Besides the novelty, the snow tires allowed the patrons to push their grocery carts with relative ease, even during the wicked worst of Wisconsin winters.

Jenny wrote other stories as well.

I remember another was about her theory that God created humans in His image and likeness as a means of signing His autograph. When someone died, Jenny claimed, it was God giving His autograph to a fan club member somewhere in this rather distant and obviously vast universe.

That short story was published in the school underground newspaper. That's where I read it. Everyone read it because we all eagerly anticipated the latest edition of *Freedom's Finest,* which was a subversive unauthorized newspaper with the major claim to fame that WE DON'T PRINT THE FOOTBALL SCORES AND WE DON'T CARE WHO IS ELECTED HOMECOMING QUEEN! It wasn't exactly "don't tread on me," but we all got the message. Such were the times.

Mr. Cullet, a biology teacher and short story critic, took issue with Jenny's story, labeling it "total guano" in each of his class lectures that week. Ironically, his protestations only generated more interest from even the most reclusive fan of the unofficial school paper. They were more willing to shell out the dime to sample the forbidden fruits of The Revolution contained within the pages of our *Freedom's Finest* underground paper.

TWO NECESSARY HIGH SCHOOL FLASHBACKS

The two kids who published the thing made a few bucks from that issue.

# # #

They say that time heals all wounds, but that's not true.

At our twenty-fifth class reunion in 1999, Mr. Cullet, who was decent enough to attend, once again argued with Jenny about her story. Of course, we all knew the truth: if he talked to her about the story, he didn't have to confront a former varsity football player named Junior Weston.

I don't blame him.

# # #

Junior Weston wasn't at all happy to discover that Buzz Hogey would never make it as a big-time drug dealer.

I knew Buzz Hogey as a fellow cross-country runner. Cross-country is a weird sport that involves running three miles or so through the woods and earning, ironically, the fewest number of points to win the meet.

I joined the team, figuring I had a shot because the race would be so long that, eventually, just about everybody else would drop out from sheer exhaustion and I could keep running long enough to earn a varsity letter. In my sex-addled adolescent mind, that meant attracting would-be females. Surely it was a sign that I could run, jump, or push someone down with a passion that studious "thinkers" could never know.

So I knew Buzz. In addition to cross-country, Buzz told stories that just were not true. They were very different from Jenny Egolenski's stories. Buzz had a problem with reality.

One time he told everyone that he was a big-time drug dealer. He said his brother Kevin grew pot in his bedroom under great big lights. He told important people in our class that he could supply them with heavy-duty drugs.

We, of course, just laughed at his story, but several members of the varsity football team took him up on his offer.

Obviously, these varsity football players had spent too much of their educational time on the gridiron, and not enough time learning to be smart. Several of these football stars, led by none other than Junior Weston, really wanted some big-time drug stuff. They wanted it enough to seek out Buzz Hogey, a well-known nobody and cross-country runner.

Poor Buzzy!

These were big-time sports stars in our school who wanted to pay attention to him, and I think Buzz genuinely wanted to make them happy.

Buzz wanted everyone to be happy.

So, instead of the real drugs he had promised, he delivered his sister's birth control pills to these eager jocks in a clandestine third-floor bathroom rendezvous, although it was totally against the athletic drug code in our school. Apparently, these football stars wanted their crack at the high school high life, such as it was. What they got was a sweaty handful of Carrie Hogey's birth control pills disguised as big-time dope. They were all in mid-birth control high when they were caught by Mr. Cullet.

Mr. Cullet reported the apparent drug deal to the principal, which caused big trouble for Junior Weston, the football star. He was suspended for the next three games.

Junior became really angry and embittered, and, I suppose, was the reason Mr. Cullet distracted himself by continuing to argue with Jenny about her story at our twenty-fifth class reunion.

He was willing to talk to anyone to avoid a confrontation with Junior.

Again, I don't blame him.

I wanted to avoid Junior, too.

CALL ME ISAAC

Shakespeare wrote, "If music be the food of love, play on."

Yes, indeed. We all need to play on.

Steven Drake, the band's bass player, showed up for practice at five. Mr. U., the drummer, was another story. He was twenty-two, quite a bit older than the others, but he had already been in other bands. His long hair hung to his waist, and he drove an old red van with the word TUG painted on its side.

"Have you ever heard of The Steel Tulips?" he asked me.

I hadn't.

"Well, we played Iron Butterfly and Vanilla Fudge. We played the heavy stuff. Before that I was in The Royal Family. We played all the British Invasion stuff: The Beatles, Stones, Kinks. Never played Herman's Hermits. Hate the pop stuff. Just won't play it. How about The Evolutionary Apes?"

I shook my head.

"What about The Furious Screams? We played everywhere. Everyone knows The Screams. They kicked me out. It was a big deal. We were all set. Somebody had a friend of a friend who knew somebody at one of the big record labels. I think it was RCA. People came to see us. They all said that we were great. Then our lead singer says the record people want us to go country. Now how can we be The Screams and sing country music? Then we're all told to get haircuts.

"'Look,' I told them, 'I don't play pop.' And then I told them that I don't play country. I also told them that I wouldn't get a haircut."

"So they kicked you out?"

"Yeah," he said. "But they never did record anything. We should have stayed The Screams and played rock music. We could have made our record the way we wanted."

He paused, reflectively.

"We were really close. We almost made our record."

Although Mr. U. claimed to be twenty-two, I think he was really a lot older than that. I met him years later in a heavy metal band called Rock 'n' Roll Heaven. at the summer solstice weekend named, ironically, Druid's Snowfest. Before the show, he told me that it was his twenty–second birthday. He still had hair down to his waist.

Apparently, his Rock 'n' Roll Heaven. had recorded a few songs. One of the songs, "Last Exit Ramp," had been played to death on a local radio station. I watched him play that day and believed he was indeed twenty-two.

He was great.

Unfortunately, the audience was a family crowd who wanted to hear familiar good-time music. Parents with kids lifted on their shoulders kept yelling for British pop tunes of the sixties and American country rock favorites.

Poor Mr. U.

One drunken man, who was a fan of the band, yelled out and requested their one big song, "Last Exit Ramp." The guy meant well, but he was too intoxicated to notice that the band had just played the song.

Mr. U. never stayed very long in any band. That's where he earned his name. He told me that he never stayed long enough for anyone to remember his name, so everyone just called him "Hey You."

Hence the name.

"Hey you," Steve, the bass player, said to him. "Let's get this Setter Dance thing going."

Mr. U. sat on his drum stool.

"Sure man," he said. "I have a cousin who has a friend who knows somebody at Warners. This is the one. This is the band that's going to make a record. I can feel it."

He then started to sing "Let's get this Setter Dance thing going" to the tune of "The Banana Boat Song."

He always did that.

He took the last bit of conversation, usually just some meaningless snippet of words, and sang that one line to some worn out melody. Then he would always ask, "Would you buy this song if some famous person sang it?"

It was all a good-natured joke. That said, our Mr. U. played rock music with his heart and his life. Even years later, at our local Druid's Snowfest, with people yelling for the easy way—people yelling for pop and country—he still pounded his beat with the anger of youth clinging with fingertip touch to its innocence in the cold face of the stone hard reality of the human race and its love of hypocrisy, complacency, and million-selling, platinum gold, radio-friendly, just plain awful music.

Good for him.

Mr. U. can be any age he wants. That's all right with me.

Steve Drake, the bass player, and Richard had been friends since elementary school. They went way back. They really did build castles. Not in the air, mind you, but in the neighborhood park sandbox.

Let's face the truth, though: everything erodes.

Castles in the sand are probably a bit less ephemeral than those in the air; but sand structures can be kicked apart, washed away by the tides of days as they seep back and forth, or just forgotten and left as is, and in time as was, and finally, no more.

There once was trust between Richard and Steve.

Sometimes good childhood friends have very little in common as each person finds who he is, or what he wants. Unfortunately, there are always so many memories; and it is often hard to say the right words, which, of course, express a sad good-bye.

That's the way I saw it between the two of them, although I know they really didn't want it that way.

Steve Drake wanted to be famous. Ralph Waldo Emerson said the greatest people have the shortest biographies. That may be true, but I don't believe Steve was very likely to quote Emerson. He wanted the longest biography in the book. Too bad for him. He didn't have it in him to write a very long story.

Too bad for Richard as well, because he did. Richard had the talent to write a very great story and a couple of good songs. And Steve knew it.

Molly, the beautiful woman of my sudden infatuation, played the necessary role in a band with a girl singer. The audience all fell in love with her; and hence, we liked the band. Molly was our calling card, our attraction. She was the Queen of all our hearts, and my heart was the first in line.

Allow me to digress.

I can speak for a generation of young men who weren't lost to the gas and trenches of World War I, or caught up in the bloody necessity of Hitler's defeat, or even for that matter, lost to the tragedy without any redemptive final soliloquy called Vietnam, of which the initial optimism of my playground years had turned to bitter bile in the throat of my teenaged existence when I, too, came of age.

This was the time when the fathers of our dear country, just like the Biblical patriarch Abraham, took their sons to the altar of war, the altar of death, and in a moment had to decide if the purpose of youth is sacrifice or nurture.

Should we, as adults, send our kids to die, or should we be the protectors of our youth? Teach your children indeed! Call me Isaac. God the Almighty, beating Pink Floyd to the punch by several thousand years, called out to those who wished to teach with bayonets of war and said with burning bush intensity to leave the kids alone.

Call me Isaac.

God, was I lucky.

Like the others who came of age in 1974, I was saved by a much higher calling. Thanks to the Gospel of John Lennon, we all knew that, for the most part, love was all anyone needed.

Diamond rings no longer meant a thing, and we lived to find love, freedom, and great music—not that we really knew what any of that stuff was. We were just really happy that the draft board wasn't looking for us.

PRE-RAMBLE ON

That old soldier at the war museum in London slowly sipped his tea.

He looked around the cafeteria. There were two punk rockers who sat at a table and swore at each other.

It was 1977 and punk rock was the rage, so one of them wore a T-shirt that read "Anarchy in the U.K." The other wore a shirt with the word "DESTROY!" scribbled in black marker on the front. Both of them had Mohawk haircuts.

One of the lads had a big safety pin in his nose. He poured his tea on the floor of the cafeteria.

They both laughed.

"What do those two know?" the old man asked.

"They're just punk rockers," I explained. "They're just like that. They hate everything. That's what they do."

"Kids," he said. "What do they know? That kid wants to destroy. Yeah. I stabbed a man. I killed him. What do they know about destruction?"

He paused.

"They can wear the shirts. They can listen to their rock music. But I've done it. Young fools like those two don't belong in Hell. War belongs in Hell.

"I belong in Hell.

PRE-RAMBLE ON

"Destroy. Hell. I've shaken hands with a dead man. I've shaken hands with death so many times that I've memorized the color of the dirt beneath his broken nails. I know the pattern of the bloodless veins that have collapsed into his lifeless skin. My finger has traced the sunken patterns of those veins that mirrored the very trenches in which we decayed daily in the dirt."

His voice rose.

"I've kissed the hand. I've begged to live, and I've begged to die. I've felt the heat of blood. I've smelt blood."

He looked me in the eye.

"Blood has a smell but it doesn't have a sound," he said. "For Christ's sake, I've urinated in the blood of people who were my friends. I didn't have a choice. The blood was just there and it smelled, and I just had to urinate. There was dirty blood in every dirty puddle."

The old man eyed the two punk rockers with their Mohawk haircuts, particularly the one that had that safety pin in his nose.

"*They* never did that," he said. "They're just punks with T-shirts. They want to destroy. What do they know?"

I guess he had a point.

The whole war museum had a point.

It was as sharp as the razor-edged bayonet that sad old man had used in the trenches of Europe so many years ago. I saw in my gaseous haze of an imagination that old man, now transfigured to his former self in the trenches of battle, stab another man and lose forever the melody of a hope in Heaven.

For a magical moment, I thought that I, too, bled. I felt the warm wet drops of sudden stigmata.

But, of course, I was wrong. I had simply shuddered in a moment of fearful thought and had spilled the hot tea I was sipping on my leg.

There would be no purple heart—no sainthood—for me. Mortality revealed its finite heartbeat.

So I stared at his medals and slowly poured myself another cup of tea.

BACK TO THE BAND

Richard was the leader of the band.

He was the kind of person who could wander off, saying he "really needed to talk to a tree for a while." We all knew he was smart, so none of us laughed about it when he did so. After a while, we all began to wonder what the trees were saying and what we were missing.

It might seem rather odd, but remember that my graduating class of 1974 was the first to avoid the televised draft lottery for the Vietnam War. We were exempt from the birthday drawing—that thread of the Fates, which would have determined the next four years of our lives. And, given the precarious nature of the Vietnam War, those years could have proven to be our final moments on dear planet Earth.

I don't mean to sound like a sighing old man, but when I hear kids today declaring their right to party, I can only think back to kids who were close to my own age, who were fighting for their right to live, fighting for the rights of their friends to live, or their brothers to live, or their uncles to live. I watched as a thousand mothers and girlfriends and sisters and nieces were all forced to watch their soldiers, their sons, their boys, wave good-bye to them.

The kids of my youth were fighting so love didn't have

to take that one last long look.

And they weren't just fighting in Vietnam. They fought in America, too. They were beaten in America. They were put in prison in America. And sometimes, they were even killed in America.

Such were the Kent State times.

Richard Lamm and his need to talk to trees sounded like Biblical wisdom when compared to the quartermaster's call for more toe tags and the silver transport coffins of my country's police operation in Vietnam, which wasn't even an official war like the wars of my uncles and fathers and grandfathers: where a rifle was actually loaded and an enemy was actually shot, where the good guys lived and were heroes, and the bad guys died because they were, of course, evil.

Vietnam wasn't like that.

It wasn't like that at all.

Our band played its music in the uneasy and vague turmoil of times when we all knew that society's status-quo soup served in our bowl as cold war leftovers wasn't what we wanted to eat. We demanded more on the menu. There had to be more to life than Iwo Jima and Normandy's bloody beaches. The soul food we wanted had more to do with Marvin Gaye than with Korea and the 38th Parallel.

I listened to The English Setter Dance's repertoire at their practice. They operated under the theory of "like it." The group either played a cover version of a song because they did "like it," or they played an original tune because nobody else played anything "like it."

They played Tull's "Locomotive Breath," The Guess Who's "No Sugar Tonight," The Who's "Won't Get Fooled

Again," the Yes acoustic song, "Your Move," and my favorite, "The Story in Your Eyes" by The Moody Blues. They also played a couple of rather obscure songs like "The Weight" by The Band and "Eugene Pratt" by an unknown group called Mason Proffit.

They played three original songs, all written by Richard. Mr. U. continued to write his one-line songs taken from random conversations. Steve would say something like, "Hey, we're running late." Then Mr. U. would mimic those words in a singsong melody resembling something popular like John Denver's "Take Me Home Country Roads." Naturally, he followed that with, "Would you buy that song if a famous person sang it?"

Of course, he was never very serious.

Richard was the real songwriter.

His first tune at this particular rehearsal was a song called "My Happiest Days." It was all about listening to those trees. Molly sang the beautiful melody and played a flute solo in the middle of the performance.

The second song they played was "Hold Me Tight," the one Richard said he had written when he was fifteen. It was the one about the two teenagers who stood out in the cold night with aching hands and aching hearts. It was rather loud, and Richard sang it with a voice that stirred butter into three-day unrefrigerated cottage cheese.

He was right, though. That song did have a great chorus. I still remember that melody as he sang:

This moment is all we've got
So praise all gods and thanks a lot.

He played the song only once or twice, so that's all I remember. But that little bit was really good.

His third song was the odd man out. It was called "Onward, Christian Canines." Richard explained that the song occurred to him late at night while he was watching a movie about El Cid, a great Christian hero, who fought the Muslim Moors in Spain. One Muslim insulted El Cid with the words, "Die! You Christian Dog!" El Cid cursed the Muslim to "eternal damnation in the fires of Hell!" Then El Cid, the Christian hero, killed the man by running his sword through the Muslim's chest, right up to the hilt, which was its outspread design, symbolizing the one true cross.

Richard said he watched this late-night show with Lola, his English setter, on his lap. He wrote the song about dogs. I really do have to agree with him. Most dogs are gentle, loving creatures who constantly forgive and turn the other jowl, so to speak, in a true Christian way. We humans, on the other hand, often trespass against our better selves by losing patience and being mean to each other and these kind loving canine creatures that are entrusted to our care.

The band finished with "Lola" by The Kinks. The setter's ears perked up when she heard the song. She stood, awkwardly, on her back paws, and then she did her dance. Without thinking, I suggested, "You should make that dance part of your show. Everyone would love it."

They all agreed.

It was my first contribution to the band.

I would live to regret those words.

REALLY GOOD COMPANY

There was a knock on the door.

"Hey! Petey! Could you get that?"

Steve was the only one who ever called me "Petey."

I was Peter J. Barooke on my high school diploma, Pete to my friends. When I was little, my mother called me PJ. When Junior Weston—the guy no one wanted to talk to at our high school reunion—almost shook my hand, he just called me Barooke. But no one, save Steve, ever called me Petey. He just did that sort of thing.

Some people are really quite good at being obnoxious.

I opened the door.

I'll always remember the slight breeze in that doorway, blowing the gentle and divine soul known as Rock 'n' Roll Randy into my life. Randy was our sometime manager and full time devotee to all things rock 'n' roll.

"Hey! Rock 'n' Roll!" Steve called out. "You're late!"

The skinny kid wearing a T-shirt that read HARD ROCK CAFÉ VENUS just smiled and said, "The Beatles, man. 'In My Life,' man. Pink Floyd, man. The Floyd. Free, man. 'All Right Now.' You know. 'All Right Now.' Van der Graaf Generator. Hammill. You know. Peter Hammill. Marc Bolan. The Kinks. 'You Really Got Me.' Uriah Heep.

'Look at Yourself,' man. 'Sweet Freedom.' You know. 'Easy Livin'.'"

"That's too bad," Steve replied.

"Yeah, man," he continued. "'Free Bird.' You know. Skynyrd. 'Sweet Home Alabama.' You know. 'Sweet Home.'"

I looked at Richard and raised my eyebrow.

He translated, "Randy said he forgot a Uriah Heep tape and he had to go back to get it."

I was amazed.

"You'll figure it out," Richard said. He paused. "And you know how it is."

"How what is?" I didn't understand.

"That Skynyrd part," Richard explained. "That's what he meant. He said, '"You know how it is.' He's late because he wanted to hear the Heep tape."

I looked at Rock 'n' Roll Randy and said, "Neil Young and Tangerine Dream." These were the only two names that came to mind at the moment.

Randy grinned and nodded his head several times. "Neil Young, man," he said, continuing to nod. "Tangerine Dream. The Dream, man. 'Alpha Centauri.'"

And that was that. We were friends—rock 'n' roll outlaw blood-brothers. Of course, our friendship only existed at the Hard Rock Café on Venus, but that was all right with me. Friendship is one of the rarest of coins minted in the universe.

Rock 'n' Roll Randy spoke rock 'n' rollese. Everyone else seemed to understand him. I didn't, but everyone else did. It was a foreign language they never taught in high school. The Revolution was never part of the curriculum of my youth. So I did the best I could and tried to remember the names of all the bands I knew.

"The Stones," Randy said, *"Sticky Fingers.* And Mott the Hoople, man. 'All the Young Dudes.' You know. 'Stairway to Heaven.' Zeppelin."

I looked at Richard again.

He translated, "Randy says that he's set up a gig for Saturday night."

"Where we playing?" asked Steve.

"Yes, man. 'Roundabout' man. 'Your Move.' 'Close to the Edge.' Totally 'Close to the Edge.' You know? 'Starship Trooper.'"

Mr. U. kicked his bass drum. He just wanted to play music.

"He's just set us up to play The Sled Shed," Steve complained. "That's just a show in Hell. It's just snowmobilers without any snow."

Richard spoke up. "Well," he said, "at least it's not a strip joint. Some bands play the strip clubs. At least it's not that bad. That's the end of the world."

"Let's just play," Mr. U. said, impatiently. "We just have to play and everything will be all right."

Molly broke out in an impromptu rendition of the Stones' "Satisfaction." All the others joined in as she sang. It was then I noticed that, despite all the personalities involved, this band—this group of people—liked very much to play music together.

In the midst of the vast differences and sarcastic comments, and even Mr. U.'s stupid songs, something came together in the flow of the music when each note needed another to produce a melody. Each instrument oddly avoided the other and filled a hole left in the wake of noise left by somebody else.

I could feel the familiar kinship between Richard and Steve. Molly sang so beautifully because she was in love with Richard. Mr. U. just beat the pulse of life a bit harder than most people. Like a Frankenstein creation of a band, The English Setter Dance came to life. The sparks flew, and I laughed and danced because that's how I felt when these four people produced this unity called music.

Even better, it was rock music, and it had a great backbeat.

"Totally Bad Company," Rock 'n' Roll Randy said. "'Feel Like Makin' Love.' 'Can't Get Enough.' 'Deal With The Preacher.'"

It suddenly occurred to me that I knew Rock 'n' Roll Randy.

I remembered seeing him at school in the principal's office, screaming at the poor guy about Deep Purple and The Who and Pink Floyd. At the time, I had passed it off as one of a billion images from a typical day at school. Some teacher probably told me about the sinking of the battleship *Maine*, which was the justification for another one of our country's wars. But really, who cared?

It's all such a blur.

But I suppose everyone, including our poor principal who had to listen to Rock 'n' Roll Randy scream, tried really hard to figure out if there was anything left to really care about in the world. Teachers seemed to care about vacations. The cheerleaders seemed to care about football and big football players. A friend of mine named Kolby Kolbacheck ran for class president.

Kolby formed The Birthday Party and printed—at his own expense—signs detailing all the wrongs in the school and his proposed solutions, which, at the time, made a lot of sense. Of course, he lost to a guy named Craig Hanso, who really wanted to date a girl named Norma Rose Luffy. I also remember a guy named Jim Milligan, who had really long hair. He came to school one day and told everyone who would listen about the poverty in a country called El Salvador. He said the people there were really poor and we should do something to help them. He even organized car washes to raise awareness and money for the cause. It was a big deal for a while. Even the custodians in the school were impressed. I attended the benefit car wash on a Saturday with a certain amount of authentic zeal. I was attempting to quell a newly acquired sense of guilt and responsibility. It was a great day. People from school showed up to wash cars and save the world.

During a break in the car washing, I chanced a wide-eyed political comment to Kevin "Crash" Hogey, the brother of Buzz Hogey, who, if you recall, once brought his sister's birth control pills to school and tried to pass them off as big-time drugs.

"I think," I told Kevin "Crash" Hogey, "I think if we wash enough cars that maybe, you know, maybe we can change the world."

He laughed.

"Change the world?"

He laughed again.

"Man," Kevin "Crash" Hogey said, "I'm lucky if I change my underwear once a week. Who cares about all this suffering in the world stuff? I failed geography class twice."

My world paused on its axis.

"No, man, I'm here for that!" He pointed to several Carly Simon clones in pleasantly revealing swimsuits, who were bent over the hood of the car they were washing.

My heart sank when he said that, as if I had just shown up at a cancelled party.

Kevin's comment hurt in a uniquely painful way, like a drill bit chasing a deep cavity. Starving people don't really just go away. I suppose television stops showing pictures and talking about them, but the kids are still hungry even if we stop having car washes. Kids are hungry even when the girls stop wearing bikini swimsuits.

I suppose that was why the band was suddenly so important to me. Richard and his dancing setter band made me care about something. I cared about that silly Revolution, I suppose. It was exciting. It made me want to wash cars again. It made me forget about Kevin's comment and realize that, yes, every now and then, there are some things worth worrying about.

I wanted desperately to be part of their English Setter Dance's music because they made me think about Jim Milligan and all his crazy long-haired ideas about trying to change the world.

If, indeed, there was a Hard Rock Café on Venus, my compass was certainly set, and I was all ready to go.

KARMA AT FIRST SIGHT

"Once you start playing the strip joints, it's the end of the world," Richard had said. "It's the end of the line for a band."

"The End of the World! Wow! The End of the World!"

Mr. U. was excited.

"I played in that band," he said. "We were The End of the World. Believe me! We were totally into The Beatles. We were the only band who could play *Rubber Soul* for a set. We played the whole album. Record company people came to see us. One was from Atlantic. That's the big-time. He was going to give us a record deal with Atlantic Records. I wanted to meet Led Zeppelin, but then the lead guitarist started dating a backup singer from some country band and left us to go get married.

"How do you play The Beatles without your guitarist?

"So we got another guy, but he was into Kiss.

"We almost made it, but we were playing Kiss and they told me I have to wear all this make-up. But we almost made it. The End of the World. We were a great band."

Mr. U. rocked back and forth, looking out into space.

"Man! We almost got signed to Atlantic. I almost met Led Zeppelin. We almost made a record."

Meanwhile, Steve still wasn't happy about playing at The Sled Shed.

"Hey," he suggested, "we have time tonight. That bar is just down the road a couple of miles. Let's check it out. At least then we'll know how bad it is."

Richard agreed, but Mr. U. said he only went to a bar if he could play music. He was already out of the door and walking toward his van. The letters TUG on its side were shiny, and they reflected the moonlight.

"Hey, Randy!" Richard asked. "You want to come along?"

Rock 'n' Roll Randy shook his head and slid into a blues voice: "Ten Years After, man." Then he played a little air guitar. "Procol Harum. Big Star." He hummed a few notes of a familiar song. With that bit of melody, everyone was gone, except for Molly and me.

And, of course, Lola.

"So," I said, eyeing Molly and trying to act cooler than I could ever hope to be with such a beautiful woman, who was in turn looking at me with expectant eyes, willing me to say something warm enough to melt the ice between us. "So" was all I could manage. It didn't sound any better the second time.

Molly yawned.

"I think I'll just go to bed," she said. "I'm tired after all that singing."

"So," I said for a miserable third time. "How long have you been going out with Richard?"

She laughed.

"Us? Dating?" She laughed again. "No, that won't happen as long as I'm not his sacred record collection."

She stopped laughing and her smile faded.

"Not that I wouldn't mind, though. Our Richie dear is married to his music." She paused for a moment, then added, "He'll marry his Moody Blues albums before he asks me out for date."

I understood her reference.

"Hey! I really love The Moody Blues. That's a great song you sang."

She smiled and sang a snippet of "Story in Your Eyes," my favorite song from their set.

At that moment I knew the difference between a love for music and a much greater passion for a woman. I looked at this lovely person who sang such beautiful songs and found myself instantly infatuated. It was the kind of infatuation that rolled on down the highway in true Bachman-Turner Overdrive.

"Just try to get him to talk about anything else besides music," Molly said sadly. "Just try it.

"One time we were all in that stupid TUG van going somewhere to see another rock band. And then U. started talking about death. So the three of us—not Richie, of course—we all spilled our guts and fears about dying and whatever comes after. You know. Heaven or Hell. Then after miles and miles of nothing because we were talking about death, which has nothing to do with music, so after miles and miles, Richie told us all it wasn't dying that bothered him. He then said if he died—and this is his serious talk—he said if he died, it would really bother him that there would be new albums by Jethro Tull he would never get to hear."

She looked at me for reaction.

"Yeah," she said sarcastically, and shook her head. "Sure, we date."

She rolled her eyes.

"Sorry to disappoint. Dating isn't in our cards."

I wasn't disappointed.

"By the way, thanks for letting us use your place," Molly said brightly, instantly changing the subject. "When we become famous, we'll pay you with all our millions."

"Sure. No problem."

She smiled. "That will happen when I'm sixty-four. Just like The Beatles.

"And that will make Mr. U. about…"

"He'll still be twenty-two."

Molly laughed at her own joke. Then stood up and bade me good night. She turned to the setter and sang, "Come on L-O-L-A."

The setter smiled with that wrinkled lip, and then followed her into the bedroom.

I was in love twice.

It was then that my life became more than I ever dreamt it could be.

THANKS, MRS. CLEARWATER

I have suggested that it was my idea for the band to bring Lola, their dancing setter, to be part of the act. It really wasn't my idea, though. Check out the second album called *What We Did On Our Holidays* by a band called Fairport Convention. The band performs with a dog, which I believe is a German shepherd, on stage at the feet of the bass player, Ashley "Tyger" Hutchings.

The front cover of the album has a chalk sketch of the group with, I presume, the same dog who has a halo of hearts around his head. I had seen the cover in Richard's collection before I made the suggestion.

We were all anxious about playing at The Sled Shed. We were the opening act, so we arrived early, hoping to set up and practice a few songs before our set. To our absolute amazement, there was already a huge crowd waiting in tendrils of impatience outside the door.

"Do you think they're here to see us?" Steve asked.

Richard looked doubtful.

"I don't think they know we exist. We're not even on the marquee."

THANKS, MRS. CLEARWATER

He was right. The sign above The Sled Shed door simply read:

TONIGHT!!!
ALL YOU CAN EAT AND DRINK
$1.00

Mr. U. tried to push his way through the eager crowd. A guy who was standing with his whole family of six carbon copy kids suddenly pushed him back. "Look," the guy said in an angry tone, "we've been here for a long time. Go to the back of the line."

"Hey! I'm with the opening band," Mr. U. explained.

The guy's son, chubby carbon copy kid number one, suddenly chimed in.

"Unless you're the cook, or the bartender, or a waitress who wants to take our order, mister, hit the road and don't stop until you see the end of the line."

Chubby carbon copy kid number two added, "And don't pass go, and don't collect two hundred dollars."

The whole chubby carbon copy family laughed with chubby smiles.

Then a third chubby carbon copy kid asked, "Do you think they have bratwursts and cheese curds in there? Because I really like bratwursts and cheese curds."

The chubby dad patted him on the head and replied, "Don't worry. This is Wisconsin. They always serve bratwursts and cheese curds here. I think it's a law."

"I'd rather eat a bratwurst than wear a seatbelt or a motorcycle helmet!" another carbon copy said.

His mother beamed with chubby pride.

Meanwhile, we had a problem.

We were here to play music, but all of these people were here to eat and drink as much as they wanted for a buck. I remembered the band we were playing with was the progressive rock group that changed their name all the time because they played really long intellectual songs nobody ever understood or liked.

This was going to be some evening.

I found a table, front and center. I was going to watch my band play its music. Unfortunately, most of the people in the bar didn't seem that interested. I think they were still looking for the promised land of smorgasbord. Indeed, Two Rivers, Wisconsin, looked a lot like Lodi, California, that night.

I watched, with smoke in the air and glasses clinking, as The English Setter Dance came to life. Mr. U. counted time and then, with a happy ignition of noise, the band played The Who's "Won't Get Fooled Again." For all those empty stomachs in the audience, the song was, I suppose, quite appropriate. Two girls in halter tops danced on the lighted floor, and the guy next to me pointed his cigarette away from his girlfriend on the other side of his table and directly into my face.

The band played their second song: my favorite, The Moody Blues' "Story in Your Eyes." The two girls continued to dance while most of the men just watched. At the end of the song, Richard announced, "That was sung by the beautiful Molly Maloney. Thanks, Molly. We'll do another one with Molly helping me with lead vocals. It's called 'Eugene Pratt.' And it's all about the war in Vietnam that's just ended."

No one in the audience seemed to care.

THANKS, MRS. CLEARWATER

I suppose you could say the song died a death that night, just like so many soldiers. The two girls didn't seem to feel like dancing to a song about a Vietnam draft resister who told his draft board to go to hell and spent his youth in a federal prison for not wanting to kill someone he didn't even know. They sat down.

In fairness, most people in those days just wanted to forget the whole mess of Vietcong, and Hanoi, and Agent Orange, and POW's, and bombing, and Cambodia, and—very soon—Richard Nixon and Watergate.

A couple of people started to talk while the band played. At least one glass fell and shattered on the bar floor. Other people went to the bathroom. I secretly hoped the band would play another popular song, a top-ten hit, to lure more women in halter tops back to the dance floor so we could all watch them move.

But the band didn't even try.

Don't get me wrong, they played great music: Tull's "Locomotive Breath," and The Guess Who's "No Sugar Tonight." There was also "Your Move" by Yes, and, of course, The Kinks' song "Lola," which inspired our setter of the same name to prance a little bit on stage.

No one really noticed Lola as she danced, though, and the guy at the next table put another cigarette in my face.

"Play 'Free Bird!'" someone yelled.

Then I heard the sound of somebody retching his beer excess in the corner of the bar, which caused another person to throw up, apparently at the sight of the mess. Then, like a domino, everyone in the bar heard a third retching gag.

Richard tried to make a joke of the whole thing.

"Boy," he said. "That'll have to stop or, before we all know it, someone will puke in Hawaii. Then they'll have to send in the marines."

I laughed, although no one else did.

Richard tried to explain.

"Remember," he said, "the domino effect was the way the generals talked us into the war in Vietnam. Well, we lost that war, but, you know, if those generals were right, then there should be communists right here in Two Rivers. Let's see." He looked hard at the audience. "Are there any communists out there?"

Two barflies yelled and raised their fists, probably because their sort just wanted to drink and raise fists at any opportunity. I watched as they both poured another beer.

Everyone else laughed, except for one man who sat at a table all by himself. From my front row seat, I looked at this solitary man whose eyes revealed he understood the joke, even if he wasn't laughing. The solitary man had one arm missing, and the sleeve of his green army coat was pinned to the shoulder. He didn't laugh at all.

I didn't understand the look on his face then; but now, years later, I think I do.

Steve was mad, so he swore.

A few people in the crowd cheered. Apparently they liked his dirty words.

So he swore again.

They cheered again.

The band launched into "The Weight," then "Hand Me Down World," and a quiet Led Zeppelin song called "Battle of Evermore," with a great vocal duet by Molly and Richard. Then it was time on the playlist to hit a few band originals, or, rather, Richard's songs, and pass them off as tunes by almost famous groups the audience did not know. Judging by the crowd, especially those throwing up in the far corner, it would not be too difficult.

But just at that moment another patron blew cigarette smoke out of his mouth and yelled, "Hey! Play some country music! I wanna hear some country music!"

Mr. U. kicked his bass drum. Hard.

The guy dragged on his cigarette again and yelled in a slurred voice, "I wanna hear some country! Play 'Desperado!' I wanna hear 'Desperado!'"

Mr. U. looked angry.

"Hey, man," he said, "why don't you check back into 'Hotel California?' I think they're waitin' for you."

The drunk smoker only smiled.

"Yeah! The Eagles! The Eagles rule!"

Mr. U. had had enough.

"All right!" he said bitterly. Then he sang in a singsong bad southern accent, "I'm senging a rea-ea-lly stupid song with a country acc-sant so you'll like our muz-zac a lo-hot. So take it eazzay." He laughed mockingly. "Hey! Would you buy that song if Conway Twitty sang it?"

Truthfully, the guy probably would have. He stood up and pointed two fingers, which still embraced a cigarette, and took a long sip form his beer. "Now! That's music," he said. Then he sat down and nursed his beer, apparently quite content with Mr. U.'s country song.

Richard looked at me as I sat at the front table. He raised his eyebrows as if he'd just had an epiphany — inspiration, I suppose. Then he played the first chords of "Onward, Christian Canines," but Steve broke a bass string, swore, and stopped playing.

The band stopped.

It was a dangerous and sudden stop.

Molly looked at Richard, waiting for his cue.

After a short pause, the audience seemed to get uncomfortable. Although they had shown very little interest in the music all evening, suddenly they were yelling for a song.

Go figure.

So Richard, needing to fill time until the string could be replaced, stepped to his mike and introduced a new song I had never heard. He would do that sometimes, just show up with something new, something really great.

"This is a song that I wrote," he said. "And I guess I'll do it by myself while we're waiting here. It's called 'Thanks, Mrs. Clearwater,' and it's about an old woman who worked in a big department store in Green Bay when I was about sixteen years old. She played records for me, and I think she was pretty great."

It turned out to be a lovely song. Molly tried to smooth out the unfamiliar lyrics by singing a gentle harmony in the background. I like to think, even after all these years, that the crowd's silence during the performance quietly revealed their enjoyment of the song.

Sometime later, Richard told me a little more about his dear Mrs. Clearwater. Of course, that wasn't her real name. Richard said he never knew her real name. He never asked. She always played records by her favorite band, Creedence Clearwater Revival. So he gave her that name.

In those days — the times before record specialty shops in malls and "head" shops in narrow back alleys of big cities — record albums were sold exclusively in big department stores. Richard told me Mrs. Clearwater was this seventy-something old lady who worked in the fourth floor record department of Pranges—an otherwise boring department store in downtown Green Bay.

Richard spent most of his free time looking through the album selection. Interesting music was just starting to hit the stores. He would always ask her about some album like Pink Floyd's *Atom Heat Mother*, with its iconic cow looking back at the prospective buyer; or *Argus* by Wishbone Ash, showing an ancient Greek warrior staring at a distant flying saucer; or *Foxtrot* by Genesis, displaying a woman with a fox head drifting away from hunters while standing on an iceberg. These records had intriguing cover art, and just looked really interesting. Richard would ask Mrs. Clearwater about these albums, and she would reply with something like, "That one does look good, doesn't it?" Then she would open the shrink wrap, saying that she was allowed to "open a few now and then." She would take her own favorites, like Creedence's *Green River*, off the record player and play these strange records while Richard listened.

But "Thanks, Mrs. Clearwater" was about much more than that.

Once when Richard was in the fourth floor record department checking out the new releases, he saw the store manager yelling at old Mrs. Clearwater and pointing to a rather large stack of albums, which were opened and therefore not returnable, resting on the front counter. The pile of albums included Pink Floyd, Wishbone Ash, Genesis, King Crimson, Yes, and all the others she had allowed him to play because they did "look good."

Richard said he stopped dead in his sixteen-year-old tracks, some distance from the store manager. Although his back was to Richard, the guy spoke loudly enough to allow almost anyone in the area to hear his heated words. Richard said Mrs. Clearwater saw him standing there. He watched as she glanced at the stack of offending records. She then looked back again at Richard... and winked.

The song was about that wink. It was a lovely song about a lovely old woman who winked at Richard, to let him know that everything was going to be all right.

The show at The Sled wrapped up with two more songs. We were all really tired by then and disgusted with the performance. The drive back to the cabin was quiet. Mr. U. probably made up a few songs, and Steve uttered a few swear words.

Richard couldn't sleep that night, so he wandered off with Lola, explaining that he needed to talk with a few trees. When he didn't return after a while, Molly wandered off with the intent to "bring him back home."

Then she was gone too long, so I decided to follow suit and find them both.

It wasn't difficult.

They were sitting by the Lake Michigan shore, and had started a small fire that quietly sparked in the darkness of the silent night. The only sound was the beautiful rhythm of the waves lapping the shore pebbles, like a huge slobbery dog just being friendly to a stranger.

Nature at night is like that.

"Am I interrupting anything?" I asked.

"Just anger," Molly replied.

THANKS, MRS. CLEARWATER

Richard, however, didn't say a word.

I sat down with them in the quiet sand. The lapping of the waves sounded sad and lonesome. They were the only whisper in the lonely night, and everything—even a whisper in the night—needs a companion with whom to share the immense joy and sorrow of the universe.

"Is it all right to interrupt anger?" I inquired.

"Sometimes."

"How about tonight?"

"Sure," Molly said. "It's just that Richard thinks the band was awful tonight. What do you think?"

"You were great," I emphasized. "It just wasn't your crowd. They were only there to eat as much as they wanted.

"But I think they all liked your Mrs. Clearwater song," I added.

I heard the sound of Lola splashing around in the lake. Richard watched her, not looking at Molly or me. "Yeah," he said. "But that was just my song. It's not the same as when the whole band is together. Then it's one for all. It's like something comes alive. We bring something to life: something bigger, some creation much better than just my song.

"That's what I want."

He paused.

"And that didn't happen tonight."

Richard's disappointment reminded me of my cousin Tommy—he who listened to weird German hippy Tangerine Dream music and ended up changing the packages of Ray-O-Vac batteries on the shelves of a discount chain store instead of changing the world. It occurred to me that Richard's Revolution, a Revolution where each individual adds his two cents of a personality to the collective band account, might just be a Revolution worth all the bother.

The three of us rested in the soft beach sand. Lola emerged from the water and nestled against Richard's legs. All of us, even Lola, looked at the stars, the very same stars that have witnessed the very same human despair for a million years. Why build castles when stone walls always fall apart? Why share secrets with friends when they are always revealed to others? Why hold on to love when, even in its best attire, love will only last for the duration of a lifetime, which is not a very long time.

The patient stars listened as Lola barked.

Then they watched as we one-by-one fell asleep on the beach.

Molly snored.

It rained that night, and in the morning we were not only wet, but we also found that Mr. U. and Steve had joined us at some point during our slumber and had decided to share our sleepy beach.

Molly laughed at Mr. U.'s long sandy hair.

Only Lola had the sense to trot back to the cabin during the night.

We found her curled and dry on the mat in front of the door. She, at least, had enough sense not to play rock 'n' roll and sleep in the rain.

I never know what to think of rain.

Sometimes it brings new life, and sometimes it's an omen of ill fortune.

I guess it's a lot like Richard's Revolution. They each make the other a bit more special.

Without new life, death is simply sad. Without death,

THANKS, MRS. CLEARWATER

new life is without magic — the magic of wise voices of the past, now gone, but still urging us on, urging us to write a new song.

ADVICE FROM A WEED

By the way, we did stay to watch the headlining act, All You Can Eat and Drink, which was the band formerly known as The Lactose Tolerant and, before that, The Push-Snowblowers.

Thankfully, the lead singer did not dress in his magician's costume. Instead, he appeared on-stage dressed as a huge weed. He wore a green stalk and yellow dandelion head-piece. Root tendrils flowed across the platform on which he stood from the bottom of his green weed stalk body.

He introduced the first song, appropriately titled "Dandelion Whine." It really wasn't about dandelions, *per se*. Instead, we all listened as the gigantic lawn growth sang Jenny Ego's lyrics about alien abductions.

According to the song, alien abductions are really nothing more than an opportunity to participate in a cosmic quiz show. We like to think we humans are the only ones abducted by the aliens, but that's just not true, Jenny Ego's song lyrics informed us. All sorts of species from Earth are taken for the cosmic quiz show. Humans are the only ones who ever really make a big deal of it.

The first part of the song introduced the three characters in the quiz show. They were an old oak, a dandelion, and a human named Doug. The characters were asked to brag about themselves. The song changed tempo as each character was introduced, reflective of each character's personality.

Doug, the human, was represented by loud, heavy rock. He told everyone how great it was to be human, and of course, earned five thousand points!

The old oak, on the other hand, just stated he was proud to give a little shade and be a nesting area for beautiful birds. The keyboard player provided the musical backdrop for the oak, which sounded a lot like a church hymn.

Finally, the guitarist, who had been standing in the shadows of the stage during the organ solo, stepped forward armed only with an acoustic instrument. I recognized him immediately.

The Clap was back!

Apparently, The Clap's differences with the band over the lactose name were safely put aside and all was well. I was happy about that, and I watched him gently finger-pick a sad melody.

Of course, no one in the place really liked all this progressive rock, but at that moment there was a bit of an attentive silence in the crowd, a smattering of polite acknowledgment that the band existed and was there to entertain them. Mind you, it was only for a moment, but it was a moment that can never be taken from the band. Sure, those tiny victories come and go, like the divine buzz of the passing bee; it is heard just for a moment while digging in the garden, but, in the end, the memory lingers, if any of us care enough to look or listen silently enough to find them.

The lead singer, who was still dressed like a weed, sat next to The Clap and sang a slow, sad story. His dandelion weed character was the third and last contestant in the quiz show. He apologized, as the dandelion, for not saying very much. But he confessed to having a sore throat and a severe headache due to the recent heavy dose of herbicide.

He said the owner of his yard wanted beautiful grass, so the chemicals were thick and strong, the kind that didn't wash away in the first rain. He said he knew humans spent time and money to get rid of him, so he felt bad, and just wished that humans would have something more to show for all their trouble.

The dandelion had a friend: a laboratory mouse who had been given fifty cigarettes each day to smoke. The mouse had, of course, developed several large cancerous tumors that were slowly killing him as a result. The mouse, the dandelion sang, didn't like these tumors, and they hurt him a lot, but he held on to the hope his laboratory death might do some good for the humans, especially those who insist on smoking too many cigarettes every day. At this point, the singer coughed several times and apologized for being such a useless and expensive bother.

The Clap continued playing his lovely guitar piece.

The rest of the band emerged soon after to finish the song. It was all quite dramatic. The song lyrics revealed the really smart aliens who put on this cosmic quiz show decided to award first prize to the contestant who scored the fewest points.

Doug, who had earned five thousand points, finished in last place. He lost to the old oak, and he lost to the lowly dandelion, who had a laboratory mouse with many large tumors as a friend.

Four or five people applauded after the song was

finished. One of the chubby boys suddenly yelled, "I want a bratwurst! I want a bratwurst right now!"

The lead singer of the band, still dressed in his weed costume, laughed and said, "We seem to have a request for a song. Sure! We can play that one."

He turned and said something to the rest of the band. They all laughed.

"Yeah!" he said, turning to face the audience again. "This next song was once called, 'A Cash Crop,' but now, because of popular demand, it's known as 'A Bratwurst.'"

The Clap tore off an explosive opening riff, similar to "American Woman" by The Guess Who, but much faster. The entire song lasted only a few minutes, which was odd for this particular progressive rock group.

Once again, Jenny Ego's lyrics explained that we humans were specially created by the same really smart aliens who played the cosmic quiz show as a means of producing irony, which was, like gold to a western man, the basis of their economy. We humans have the odd combination of hopeful bravado and self-centered stupidity that is a good chemical equation for the sudden and often humorous reversal of expected results known as irony. We humans are, to these really smart aliens, what the California gold rushers called the mother lode.

The song could have been a hit single. It was short and had a catchy chorus:

Feed those humans really well,
Just like animals in the zoo.
Grow that irony really fast
And make a profit for me and you!

A large number of people in the audience clapped along with the song because it had a great beat. Even the chubby family seemed to like it.

"Thanks a lot!" the lead singer said, wrapping up the song. "Now, we're going to play a really long song about space travel and colonization of planets. It's about an early space flight that nobody likes to talk about because it was so secret.

"See, before they sent men into space, they sent two dogs to land on the moon. But they missed. The two dogs just kept traveling farther into space. And, as far as I know, they're still up there somewhere.

"They were dachshunds.

"You know, they needed little dogs with little legs to fit into the spaceship. Their names were Otto and Fritzy. This is their song, and it's also our song. It's called 'We Came in Peace for All Mankind.'"

The Clap laughed.

"It's good to be back," he said to the singer.

The singer was right.

The song was really long.

People just got up and left.

That was a shame because "We Came in Peace for All Mankind" turned out to be the most interesting song they played. It was all about the two dachshunds who ventured past the moon and somehow traveled through the universe and met different life forms. They tried to steal precious metals, money, jewels, and women from the various other planets that contained life.

Otto, in true canine form, always urinated on each planet. That was his way to announce he had claimed the planet as his own.

We humans did a similar thing every time we bumped into a new continent.

And we, too, always came in peace.

We always do that.

The band finished their set with the song about aliens listening to Bachman-Turner Overdrive and crashing into Roswell, New Mexico. About ten people had stayed for the entire show. Later, I talked to the lead singer as he stood outside the bar and watched the equipment being loaded into their truck.

He was still wearing the weed costume.

"I liked the show," I said. "I saw you guys when you were The Push-Snowblowers."

"I remember you," he replied. "Thanks for coming. We're playing again next week."

"As All You Can Eat and Drink?" I asked.

"No, of course not. We'll be either Miss Nude USA or The Ice Bowl Highlights. We'll have to see about the crowd."

I was about to tell him I thought the names were good choices when I was interrupted. A drunken man, who had stayed for the entire show, decided he was capable of driving.

Unfortunately, he was wrong.

I watched as he drove his car into the equipment shed, right through the wooden door.

"Ouch!" the weed singer said. "I bet that hurt."

Then we watched as the drunken man tried to reverse his car. The spring of the shed door had lodged itself under his front bumper and would not let go. It tugged at the car as the drunken man accelerated.

Soon enough, the spring stretched out to its maximum length and held firm.

"Ouch!" the lead singer said again.

The drunken man slammed down the gas pedal one more time.

Then the spring snapped.

We watched as the car broke loose and sped backwards across the gravel parking lot until it hit a tree. The drunken man appeared stunned, then got out the car and examined the damaged bumper that was wrapped around the tree.

He swore, and then awkwardly stumbled toward us.

"You know," he said in a slurred voice, "I woke up today and said to myself... I said to myself... 'I don't want to get drunk today.' But you know what I did today?"

"You got drunk," I replied.

"That's right!" he said, examining me with bleary eyes. "I got drunk. Then I said to myself... I said to myself... 'If I get drunk, I don't want to drive.' But you know what I did today?"

"You got drunk and you drove," I surmised.

"That's right!" the drunk said. "I drove my car into that shed."

"I know."

"I said to myself," he said. "I said to myself this morning, 'If I get drunk and I drive, I don't want to hit anything.' But you know what I did today?"

"You hit that shed and then you hit that tree." I was onto him.

"That's right! I hit the shed and then I hit that tree."

He shook his head sadly.

"I didn't want to do any of this."

ADVICE FROM A WEED

He shook his head again.

Then he walked away.

I watched as he left his car there, the bumper still wrapped around the tree. There was a sticker on it that read, NIXON'S THE ONE! It was crinkled and ragged, just like the bumper. The drunken man walked down the road.

He disappeared in the distance.

No one would mistake him for Tom Joad.

"That was worth the price of admission," I said to the lead singer.

"But the guy's right," he replied.

"What do you mean?"

"Well, he's right about everything," the singer explained.

"He's just a drunk who crashed his car into that tree."

The lead singer was not convinced. "You should listen to the guy."

"But he's just a drunk."

"Sure, but he just explained everything you need to know."

"So what's everything I need to know?" I asked.

The lead singer, who still wore the weed costume, smiled and said, "Always be sure to give the people what they don't want.

"I love being a singer in a band." He paused. "But I really love... I *really* love being the weed in the garden."

I suddenly realized that this lead singer with all of his odd progressive rock songs had, indeed, managed to leave the temple. He knew things I did not know. He was part of The Revolution.

I was envious.

He gave the people what they did not want.

He knew the real reason people poisoned the dandelions in their yards every year.

TWO MORE NECESSARY
HIGH SCHOOL FLASHBACKS

I don't blame Mr. Cullet for wanting to argue
with Jenny Egolenski about her story claiming we
are all nothing but God's autographs. I don't blame
him at all because, in truth, he just wanted to avoid
a confrontation with Junior Weston, the star football player who was suspended for three games after
he was caught buying Carrie Hogey's birth control
pills. I wanted to avoid a confrontation with Junior
Weston, too.

In eighth grade, I caught a last-second game-
winning touchdown pass. It was the sort of thing
that should have been gold currency to a young
teenager on a Friday night of certain celebration.

But it wasn't, because Junior Weston had been
the defensive back guarding me when I caught that
touchdown pass. For a moment, I was a hero. Our side
of the crowd went nuts. You could hear them screaming from the field.

I was happy.

I was really happy.

It's great to be a football hero.

Then the dark side of fame quickly manifested

itself. Junior Weston, in an apparent moment of conciliatory gamesmanship, ran close to me. He was close enough to shake my hand. He smiled. Then, with a malicious grin, he said, "Hey Barooke. You'll pay for that catch. You'll pay for that touchdown, if it's the last thing I do."

His voice took on a more evil edge.

"I'm going to make you pay."

He ran off.

He never did shake my hand.

Junior, I should note, was a well-known tough guy around the area. He was a hockey player before hockey became a popular spectator sport. His only redeeming quality was that he always kept his word. Unfortunately, he only gave his word when he promised to beat the daylights out of somebody.

So, I knew that I was in trouble.

I confess. I lived in mortal fear of Junior Weston for years. He and I even ended up at the same high school, which was torture. I lived the nightmare of masculine adolescence: this well-known tough guy who played football and hockey was waiting for me; he was plotting his revenge. I would suffer for the rest of my life because of an eighth grade football catch.

Eventually the situation resolved itself, at least for a while. It happened one day as I waited in line to buy a Snickers Bar from a candy vending machine. Junior appeared out of nowhere and suddenly put his hand on my shoulder and said, "I know who you are."

My heart stopped.

I turned ice cold in panic and pulled the wrong candy bar selection knob. Now I was not only going to be beaten to a pulp, but I also had to settle for a Payday because I had pulled the wrong knob.

I never even liked Payday candy bars.

"Yeah," Junior said with his hand on my shoulder, "I know you."

"Y-You do?"

"Yeah, you're that cross-country guy. It's not much of a sport, but it's still a sport, so you gotta sign this." He handed me a piece of paper. "They won't let me play."

The piece of paper turned out to be a petition. Junior had been suspended from the football team for taking birth control pills. He wanted all the athletes in school to sign and say that he should be allowed to play.

I signed the petition.

Of course, I didn't sign my real name.

"Thanks," he said as he patted me on the back. "Thanks, I owe you one. You cross-country guys are all right. You're odd. But you're all right."

He patted me on the back again.

Well, this was all very ironic. Junior and I were suddenly good buddies united in a noble cause - a means to allow him to beat the system and play football despite his three-game suspension.

Irony is one of the few certainties of this life. It's really impossible to explain. I suppose that's why it's so hard to accept. Irony presents our own

limitations; it reveals mortality; it frames a portrait of death.

Of course, none of that makes it any easier to
accept.

Irony is like having to settle for a Payday when
your heart was really set on having a Snickers Bar.
I suppose it's all just more evidence that the lead
singer in his weed costume had it right. Indeed, give
the people what they really *don't* want.

By the way, the name I signed on Junior Weston's
petition was Jonathan Maenad, who was a sophomore
in our school. He wrote folk songs and often played
them during lunch in our cafeteria.

I said the final good-bye to high school at
a party in Sylvie Maenad's back yard. She was
Jonathan's sister. It was the night of our graduation,
and very late. We were all tired. No one wanted to go
home and leave the last party because we knew our
time of innocence-the time of Jenny's stories, the
time of Mr. Cullet's arguments, the time of birth control scandals, the time of math problems and math
solutions, the time of car washes to save the world,
the time when autumn marked our measured growth in
teen years-was sadly over.

Yes, we were tired, but no one wanted to leave
because we knew all these jigsaw pieces of our youth
were about to be assembled into the puzzle of this
thing called life.

I stood at the party in a thin moment when the
ebb of night lingers against the dim sunrise. I stood
there, alone, and watched three girls as they danced

in the warm spring air. I recognized the girls and
wished I had tried to get to know them in school. But
it was too late for that now. At that moment, everything about high school was much too late.

One of the girls was named Leslie. She was in
my math class. She was blessed with a face of simple
beauty and deep dark eyes. The wine I sipped and
the intensity of the moment made me think her white
complexion rivaled the moon.

The other two girls, Ivy and Ruby, were the
only twins in our class. They were always popular.
Everybody knew them. Ruby still wore her red satin
graduation dress, but she was barefoot so her feet
were wet with the dew of the grass. The bow of her
dress was no longer tied and hung loose around her
waist. Ivy had changed into bell-bottom jeans and a
halter top. Her hair was braided into one long pony-
tail resting between her naked shoulder blades.

Pink Floyd's *Dark Side of the Moon* was playing.
It was a popular record.

Then someone accidentally bumped the stereo
and sent the needle skipping across the vinyl
grooves until it rested, finally, on the last song on
the album. All three girls began to sing the words
to the ending song. Their voices weren't very good,
and all sorts of laughter rang out around them.

It wasn't really mean laughter, though. Life
is sometimes just mean laughter, but we were still,
somehow, on the warm side of the levee. We all liked
Pink Floyd.

I stared past the girls; I stared past Leslie's

eyes, and Ivy's bare shoulders, and Ruby's wet feet and undone bow; I stared beyond all of this and saw three falling stars. I swear. I watched as these stars ran like chalk marks on a big black board. They were there for only a moment, and then they were gone. They were just a wink in the night sky from a universe-a universe that knew what we desired but was unwilling, or unable, or maybe just not ready to satisfy our requests.

There is as much of the universe in a dandelion as there is a dandelion in the universe.

The three girls heard the others laugh, and they laughed, too. Pink Floyd's album was over, and we could hear Jonathan Maenad strumming his guitar and singing Dylan's "Just Like a Woman" from his bedroom window. I took notice of the girls as they noticed me staring at the night sky. Then they began walking toward me.

Leslie stumbled and caught herself by leaning against Ivy. She was a little drunk.

"Hey!" she said. "Hey math guy! You're cute!"

I was wrong.

She was *really* drunk.

Ruby gently touched her wine glass against mine. I looked down at her wet bare feet and the fragile ends of her untied bow that swayed with the movement of her hips.

"So, cute math guy," she asked, "what are your plans for life after high school?"

I didn't know what to say. I was shy. For some odd reason I thought about my cousin Tommy and his

weird Tangerine Dream records. He knew how to be
cool. I listened to myself as I said, "I guess I'll go
and find a revolution somewhere."

Ivy tipped her head back, laughed, and said, "An
American Revolution."

Leslie's beautiful eyes were big and round.
Her lips slowly whispered, "A Russian Revolution,
perhaps?"

Ruby looked at me under lidded eyes and spoke
in a sultry voice.

"Or how about a sexual revolution? How about
that, math boy? How about a sexual revolution? I like
sex and there's nothing wrong with a revolution, is
there?"

Then she poured some of her red wine into my
empty glass.

"I think there's a band called The Revolution,"
Ivy chimed in. "I think they play cool music."

Ruby sipped the rest of her wine.

"Promise us that math boy," she said sweetly.
"Promise you'll play in a rock band."

I saw my own reflection in her glass. I barely
recognized myself. I looked so old, in total contrast
to my photo smiling youthfully from the page in the
school yearbook.

"We all like music," Leslie said. "Tell us you
want to play music all the time. That would make us
happy."

I looked into Leslie's eyes. Then I looked at my
own reflection in Ruby's glass.

"Sure," I replied. "Anything you say."

"It's not what we say," Ruby suggested. "It's what we want. It's what we really want."

She paused and smiled. "And what we want, we really get."

Of course, I didn't know then I would soon fulfill their graduation night prophecy.

I would soon find myself as a part of Richard and Molly's dancing setter band.

And, yes, I would find I truly did want to play music all the time. I did not know then the music I played would be a million miles away from high school, and graduation parties, and math problems that tried to explain the price of an apple.

A BRAND NEW SONG

Rock 'n' Roll Randy, our sometime rock 'n' roll manager, parked his car near the cabin door. Steve was in the passenger seat. Randy rolled down his window and said, "The Guess Who, man. The Stooges, King Crimson, Savoy Brown."

"Sure," I replied.

"Foghat. You know? Caravan. Genesis. Jade Warrior. The Warrior, man."

I said, "Sure."

"Man! You know. You gotta know. Fairport Convention. The Band. Gentle Giant. The Kinks."

"Sure."

Then he handed me a cassette tape marked with a handwritten label: GREATEST SONGS, EVER! That was the extent of our conversation.

"Thanks," I said.

Steve jumped out of the car and said, "It's about time we got it together. Other bands are making it."

"What other bands?" Richard asked.

"There's a crowd," Steve complained. "There's a crowd waiting for that progressive band with the weed guy."

Richard was surprised.

"Really? What are they called this week?"

"Miss Nude USA."

Molly walked toward the car. "What about Miss Nude?" she asked.

"It's nothing," Richard said. "Steve here just wants to get famous."

"Sure," Steve suggested. "Why not change the act a little bit. I mean, let's face it. Nobody cares about what we're playing."

"So what should we play?"

"Well, first," Steve pointed at Molly. "She just stands there. She should be wearing a short skirt and jewelry and make-up. She could dance around while she's singing.

"And we should be playing country music," he added. "Everyone wants country."

"The Dillards," Rock 'n' Roll Randy said. "Poco. The Flying Burrito Brothers."

Mr. U. slapped a drumstick against the wheel of the car.

"Flying Burrito nothing!" he shouted. "Flying Taco nothing! I don't play country music!"

"Country ain't that bad."

"I don't play country."

"We could make more money."

"I don't play country."

Steve was mad. "Well, maybe you should go back to your Steel Tulip band. I'm sure you'll have people lining up to come to your show."

Rock 'n' Roll Randy muttered something about The Byrds and a Sweetheart of the Rodeo.

"Don't knock The Tulips, man! We almost made it. We were a great band."

Richard tried to keep the peace.

"We could play some Creedence. They're sort of country."

"Creedence ain't country," Mr. U. protested. Then he did the drum roll from "Fortunate Son." He smiled and proclaimed, "Creedence is God's country!"

So it was settled.

We added a few CCR songs to our act. We all liked "Bad Moon Rising" and "Proud Mary." Molly said she could dance during these songs. She never said anything about Steve's short skirt comment. But in all the time I've known her—and I've known her for a long time—I've never seen her in a skimpy dress and I've never seen her wearing heavy make-up on her face.

She just doesn't have to do that.

Richard then mentioned he had a new song. It was a bit of joke. That's what he said. He insisted it wasn't anything serious. We talked him into playing the song for us. It turned out to be one of the catchiest tunes I had ever heard. It was somewhere between The Beatles' "Eight Days a Week" and a football cheer. His new song was called, "I'm Not That Stupid To Be That Stupid."

The title and lyrics were a double entendre, a two-edged sword that could be taken as literal face value, or understood as a jovial, poking commentary on those who could only understand the literal level. In other words, you could like the song because you liked to be stupid, or you could like the song because it made fun of the people who liked the song because they liked to be stupid.

Pay your money and take your chance.

If I recall, the first verse went like this:

A BRAND NEW SONG

Sure! Kids all over the world are starving
But they're really easy to ignore.
Because I've got pizzas in the freezer,
And five cold beers in the refrigerator door.
I'm not that stupid to be that stupid,
Sure! I do what I'm told!
But I'll fight for any pretty girl's right,
To be next month's Playboy centerfold!

Was it funny?

Sure.

Was it dangerous?

Sure.

The universe is always dangerous. But, believe me, we didn't see it coming at all. Years later, I watched bright-eyed American Bruce Springsteen wannabe males all over the globe proclaiming with index fingers raised that they were all "Born in the USA!" They loved their mothers; they wanted more apple pie; and they unanimously agreed that we had kicked butt in Vietnam.

To them I answer, 'yes,' 'yes please,' and 'well, not quite.'

For crying out loud! Did they ever leave the stadium benches of the world's sports arenas to listen to the guts of that song? It was a song about a guy's brother who was killed in the war. Heaven help us. It was embarrassing that they didn't get it.

I saw the danger in that crowd later in life.

I saw the danger in their ignorance, but, believe me, at the time I just thought Richard's new tune had a humorous lyric and catchy melody.

Of course, I was dead wrong. He had that future generation pegged. He had my generation pegged. He had every generation pegged.

I wished those proud American boys would sing a wonderful Bruce Springsteen song called "Reason to Believe," instead. It's a song about a dead dog by the side of a road and a nameless man who believes if he pokes the lifeless carcass with a stick and stands there long enough the dog will rise again and get up and run.

That's a decent dream.

It's the sort of dream I'm certain my grandfather had in his heart when he left war-torn Europe for America—the land of dreams—the kind of magical place where, if we believe long and hard enough, even dead dogs by the side of the road can be reborn and start again. I just wish all the Bruce Springsteen wannabes would sing that song.

Of course, we didn't know any of this stuff back then. We were just a nothing band with a rock 'n' roll manager who could barely utter a sentence without quoting from the wellspring of his stereo speakers.

But I was happy.

Molly showed me a few chords on her Epiphone acoustic guitar. I still remember the moment when I strummed the chords to "Lodi" while she sang. That was amazing.

The band had added several Creedence songs. They were great tunes to play. Richard also brought in a song called "Waterloo Sunset" by The Kinks. Molly did the beautiful high harmony singing on that one. She could do just about everything possible to my heart, but her vocals on that song hit me physically; she made my knees bend and wobble.

A BRAND NEW SONG

Steve, for the first time, suggested a few songs as well. They were odd choices.

The first song was called "I Don't Know How to Love Him" from the rock opera *Jesus Christ Superstar*. In fairness to him, I have to admit it was well-known at the time because of radio airplay. Molly did the lead vocal on it.

Steve's other choice was "Smoke On The Water" by Deep Purple. Mr. U. loved this selection until he found out that Steve insisted on singing the song himself. It was really a bit of a plod for the band, and it was much too heavy for Steve to sing, so he just screamed his way through the words.

Richard didn't think much of the songs, but he quietly agreed to play them. They were popular songs, after all. At the time, everybody was trying to write a rock opera like *Jesus Christ Superstar,* and Deep Purple was about as big as rock 'n' roll could get.

Steve wanted to play Richard's new "I'm Not That Stupid To Be That Stupid" song. Richard refused and kept saying it was just a joke, that it wasn't intended for an audience. I guess he would be the one to know because he wrote the thing, but we all thought that it was fun to play.

And we all understood the joke.

Richard would chant the words to the song with mock intensity:

Sure! I like to beat my wife,
And I always drink way too much beer.
And mister, them are fightin' words,
Tellin' me I can't smoke in here.

I ask you: could anyone fail to catch the irony? Could anyone really be that stupid to be that stupid? Or could someone possibly just enjoy being so stupid?

THE END OF THE WORLD

We played a number of shows around the area. It was enough to earn a little grocery and gas money. But, to be truthful, the reaction from the audience was dismal. Usually, Steve swore a bit, and a few people laughed, and a few girls danced on the lighted floors. That was about the extent of our fame.

No one even bothered to notice Lola, our dancing English setter.

Molly was sick for about a week in mid-July, so we had to do the next show Rock 'n' Roll Randy had organized for us as a boys' night out; except, of course, for Lola who had to be the belle of the band that night.

The English Setter Dance was advertised as a four-piece, so the others threw me into the last-minute mix with, by my own admission, about ten chords-worth of expertise. They told me to "just stay away from the microphone when you're confused and always pretend that you know what you're doing."

Sure.

We were set to play at a place called Pandora's Box in a city called Fond du Lac, uncharted waters to us. It really wasn't that far away from our usual spots, but it was the first time we had played there. As we neared Fondy—as the locals call it—raindrops splattered on the windshield of Mr. U.'s Tug van. We could just barely read the letters on the big sign over the bar through the falling rain.

I'll never forget the marquee, visible, intermittently, through the flapping wipers of the van:

GENEVA, HOPE, LULU AND OTHER SEXY LADIES
+
THE ENGLISH SETTER DANCE
LIVE MUSIC!

"Wow!" I said innocently. "We get to open for some girl group. Maybe they're like Diana Ross and The Supremes."

Mr. U., who was at the wheel, peered through the windshield at the gray clouds.

"I doubt that," he said, and then pointed to the sky. "The rain gods don't think much of the place."

We all laughed.

"Maybe they're a country group," Richard said. "I know your rain gods. They don't like country any more than you do."

Steve spoke up. "Hey, Petey! How many chords do you know on that guitar?"

"A few."

"No," he said. "How many?"

"About ten," I admitted.

"Then I'd say that you know ten more than Geneva, Hope, Lulu, and all the sexy girls they want to bring with them.

"Can you sing at all?"

"Of course not."

"Then, my dear boy, you should maybe give that Geneva there singing lessons.

"Those ladies," he intoned, "don't know much about music."

"A strip club?" Richard asked.

Steve nodded his head.

"It's just a hunch. Call me psychic. They're what you call e-x-o-t-i-c dancers.

"You know, they're strippers."

Mr. U. wasn't happy.

"Well, I don't like it. This has nothing to do with rock music."

Personally, I clung to the hope that they were really just the name of another progressive rock band nobody liked.

Richard, as always, spoke the truth.

"We're here, everyone. Welcome to the end of the world."

"I'm telling you," Mr U. said slowly, "the rain gods don't like this place."

Just an observation: exotic dancers have funny names.

Sometimes the names are chosen to conceal their real identities. We met Hope, whose real name was Chastity, which is a really bad stripper name. We also met Geneva, whose real name was just that, Geneva. Her name worked well. We never got to meet Lulu. She was too busy trying to get customers to buy her drinks, so I don't know anything about her name.

Before we walked on the stage, we worried about what songs we could play as the background for the dancing. Thank goodness for Steve's recent additions.

"I Don't Know How to Love Him" was a slow song, and "Smoke On The Water" just had a great beat. I think it has to be the most versatile song ever written. I've changed the oil in my car to that song. I've filed my taxes to that song. I've even picked out my breakfast cereal in a mega-supermarket while listening to an orchestrated version of that song.

Mr. U. said he didn't believe in much, but he knew for certain that it was wrong to play any Creedence Clearwater Revival songs while women took off their clothes.

Most of our repertoire didn't seem to fit.

Ultimately, we figured our best bet was to play Steve's two songs over and over until someone noticed. Incidentally, with Molly gone, Steve thought he could handle the lead vocal on "I Don't Know How to Love Him."

We didn't argue with him.

Geneva befriended the band immediately and spent some time with Richard. She kept telling him about all the songs she knew by heart. She told us she was a singer and had a good voice.

Richard, for some reason, appeared to be interested.

Suddenly, I wanted Molly to be there.

I wanted to talk to Molly about all the songs she knew by heart.

Then an odd thing happened.

Just about the last person I ever would have expected to be in a place like Pandora's Box walked through the door, paid his couple of bucks admission, and sat back, waiting for the first dancer to grace the stage. It was Father Pontiac, my favorite teacher from high school.

He made us laugh while he taught us history. He was a great teacher.

I should mention that Pontiac wasn't his real name. It was something else that began with "P," but no one could pronounce it the very first day of school, so we just called him Father Pontiac. The name stuck because we genuinely liked him.

He was everyone's favorite teacher. He even had a beard and a plaid sports jacket, which, believe it or not, really mattered in 1970.

I sat at his table and talked to him.

It was a little odd being where we were, but he didn't seem embarrassed at all. He remembered me. In fact, he talked about some long lost paper I had written for his class.

Maybe school means more to the teachers than it does to the students.

Father Pontiac had left our school during my sophomore year. He was now the parish priest at St. John's in Fond du Lac.

Eventually, I had to ask him, "So why are you here? Does anybody know? Don't they care? You're a priest. This is a strip joint."

Father Pontiac sipped his Coke.

He sipped his Coke again.

"I'm always looking for a saint," he said. "I'm looking for a poet. I'd even settle for a goddess from any religion in any universe.

"Maybe she's here. Maybe she's not. You never know."

"You think she's here?" I asked.

"Sure." He smiled. "Sometimes I remember to look in the dust."

"What's in the dust?"

"Everyone."

"Everyone?" I asked.

"And words."

"Words? What words?"

"Sure. Everything is in the dust, one way or another. Everyone. Everyone's every word is in the dust."

"So what do those words say?"

He looked at me. "They tell us the truth."

"So what do they say?" I repeated. Suddenly I desperately wanted to know his truth.

"Let's put it this way." He sipped his Coke again. "As long as we're both here I can tell you." He paused, leaning in. "You see, being a priest can be dangerous."

"But you're a good priest. You were a great teacher. We all liked you. I learned so much from you."

He smiled a kind smile.

"That's just the point. And let me tell you, being a teacher is even more dangerous. It's scary. Believe me, it's scary."

"Why? Sometimes I think I would like to be a teacher. Just like you."

"Well you should. You should.

"But just remember, it's difficult when people say you're such a good teacher. They think you have all the answers. They think you are so smart and so kind. And in a way that's true. But really, it's not true at all."

He paused.

"I mean, I'm sarcastic when talking about the human race and all the things people have done. Arm chair humor. And you kids like to laugh. It's great, you know? It's really great making you laugh at all the jokes. It's easy telling the jokes. And after a while it's just as easy to tell the joke instead of telling the stuff you wanted to say before you became that teacher or preacher or whatever."

"But you were funny. I liked your jokes."

He looked at me with serious eyes.

"I didn't become a priest or a teacher to be a comedian."

"So what's the real reason? Why did you teach us?"

"It's hard to say. It was a job, I guess. But when I started as a teacher, I was so bad at it. And that was good. It's always important to know how awful you are. That makes you better. Maybe that's why I'm here. Maybe that's why I wanted to teach. I wanted to be a better person. I wanted to be a kinder person. I wanted to be a more intelligent person. I wanted to be more naked.

"Not really naked, you know? But that's the only way to be better."

"We all loved your sports coat."

He laughed.

"Yeah, that was part of the show. It was all part of the show. It's just like this." He waved his hand. "It's just like this place. It's just entertainment. That's what I did. I entertained. I never did tell you people the truth, and I'm supposed to know the truth.

"Sometimes I do. Sometimes I don't. Sometimes I'm not certain which is which.

"But my teaching had nothing to do with any of that."

He sipped his Coke.

"What should you have told us?" I asked.

"We all need to know, dear student." He looked into my eyes. "We need to know the difference between fact and fiction, and the difference between good and evil and up and down and pass and fail, and the difference between blasphemy and a few decent questions for a deity somewhere."

He looked even more deeply into my eyes.

"There was a war on, for God's sake! I should have said something. I should have told you not to go to that war, but they said we shouldn't talk about that.

"So I just told jokes and talked about history." He paused and looked at the dancer on stage. "I don't even know when to drink and when to stay sober. I don't even know enough to stay out of places like this. That's why I don't teach anymore."

I was silent for a moment. I felt like I had been thrust into the position of becoming this man's confessor.

"So," I finally said, "you come here to be with all the wicked people in a strip joint. Good and bad are simple in here."

"Oh, I don't think that's true," he said. "I don't think people in here are any more awful than anywhere else. It's just that when you're naked, it's a lot more difficult to hide the flaws. We're all naked here. Not just up there." He pointed to the stage. "We all need something. We can't get it out there. So we all come here."

"Hey! Mister rhythm guitarist!" Richard called over the small PA system. "We can't play without you!"

Steve and Mr. U. laughed.

I left Father Pontiac and took my place on stage, armed with Molly's Epiphone guitar and about six chords I could count on myself to get right most of the time.

I stepped far away from the microphone.

Then another odd thing happened.

We launched into "Smoke On The Water," which was a good song for a striptease dance. Steve screamed the vocal part. I saw Richard wince once or twice. It was that bad.

Geneva, the dancer who had befriended the band, performed her act. This was, indeed, a boys' night out.

We then did our slow dance song, "I Don't Know How to Love Him," the big hit from *Jesus Christ Superstar.*

Molly sang this song so well, but Molly wasn't here. So Steve crawled his way through the melody, which, to be quite honest, wasn't very good that night. He didn't even bother to change the pronouns to make it into a guy's love song for a girl.

We sounded so awful, like a man with a Sunday morning hangover and no aspirin in the house.

Then the odd thing really did happen.

Geneva stopped her dance and waved her arms in the smoky bar air, exasperated.

"I can sing that song better than that!" she yelled. She quickly looked around and asked another dancer, who might have been Lulu, if she would take her place on stage while she sang with the band.

"No way!" the girl yelled. "I'm not ready yet. Ask Hope. She'll do it!"

"Hey! Hope!" Geneva asked. "Could you finish my dance? I want to sing that song."

Hope smiled.

Geneva took the mike and proved she could sing as well as she could dance.

We sounded good with her on lead vocals.

Richard smiled at the end of the song. "Let's do that one again," he said.

I don't think anyone minded. Our band wasn't the center of attention anyway.

Hope, who had replaced Geneva on stage, was bathed in strobe lights; she was very beautiful, and she was removing her clothes one piece at a time. All eyes were riveted on her movements.

Then I noticed at the very front of the stage was a man in a wheelchair. Through the shutter-speed flashing lights I could see that one side of the man's face sagged terribly with rings of baggy flesh. His back was bent and humped. His legs were small and malformed as they rested in the wheelchair, and he held a folded dollar in his right hand.

Behind him, in the flashing strobe lights, I saw several signs that read: DON'T TOUCH THE DANCERS! PLEASE DON'T TOUCH THE DANCERS! IF YOU TOUCH THE DANCERS, YOU WILL BE ASKED TO LEAVE!

Apparently, they didn't want us to touch the dancers.

I watched Hope as she looked at the odd man with a folded dollar in his hand as he sat in his wheelchair. Through all the noise and flashing lights and cigarette smoke, I thought I somehow heard her whispered words.

"It's all right," she said to him. "We can break the rules. Just this once. Just for you."

The man's hand, still with the dollar firmly tucked between his fingers, gently squeezed her thigh. Then his hand rubbed her knee, and then, finally, it stroked her naked calf.

Hope smiled at his saggy face and touched his humped shoulder with her right hand. There was no sign in the place that forbade her gesture. The man's hand slowly dropped back to the side of his wheelchair.

He smiled, too.

I looked at Father Pontiac, and he looked back at me. He was still my teacher, and I was still his pupil.

Then I looked past him, out through the window of the bar. I saw the moonlit parking lot. The rain had suddenly stopped. It occurred to me that Mr. U.'s rain gods and Father Pontiac's goddesses from any universe must have been pleased — indeed, very pleased at that moment.

Hope finished her dance as we played a few more songs. I do not believe she ever took the man's dollar.

I recall one more thing about that night: Richard finally took control of the band.

We were sounding really good, and I could tell that Richard was happy. After "Smoke On The Water" had been reprised several times, Steve said to Richard, "Come on! Let's do 'I'm Not That Stupid.'"

Richard, feeling loose, played the opening chord sequence and sang the first verse, the one about not caring if children starve because he had enough pizza and beer in the fridge. Suddenly, several of the men in the audience began to bob to the infectious beat of the song and turned their chairs to look, for the first time during the night's performance, at our little setter band.

One dancer, who sat at the bar, glanced over her shoulder and nodded her head in approval of our song.

When we finished, Richard yelled, "Do 'Lola!' Come on! Let's keep this going!" The Kinks' classic had a similar infectious beat, so the audience continued to bob and weave their shoulders and necks and arms.

It was fun to watch.

Of course, right on cue, our secret weapon, our ever-faithful English setter, heard the clarion call of her song, her muse, urging all good dogs to strut their stuff.

And that she did. Quite well I might add. For the very first time, someone in the audience noticed our setter's dance.

Of course, it just had to be one of the strippers.

"Hey! She's just like a tiny dancer in that song," she called out.

Lola, our beautiful setter, balanced awkwardly on her hind legs, danced forward and grinned at her fan. Her humans were pleased, and she liked that, so Lola danced a little more. The crowd applauded her efforts. She grinned.

"Take it off!" someone yelled.

"Yeah! Sweetheart! Take it all off!"

Lola grinned again.

Then someone yelled to Lola, "Nice chest!"

To be fair to both the speaker and our own dancing dog, I had to admit that it was the truth. Setters are bred to develop a rather large chest cavity. They need large lungs for running and retrieving grouse and other upland game birds. I also believe they have a large chest area to contain their big hearts, and they need space for all their honest affection for their humans.

But, whatever the reason, the man was right. She did have a big chest.

When the song was over, the crowd applauded. That was the very first time anyone noticed our music and our dog. After that, the night just continued with more songs and a lot more stripping. Later, this guy came up to us as we took a little break.

"I just want to tell you," he said with a cigarette dangling between his lips, "I really liked that stupid song."

"Which stupid song?" Steve asked.

"You know, the one about beating my wife and drinking and smoking. We smokers have rights too. My wife always tells me not to smoke around our kids. That really gets me, you know? It's like she's asking for a beating."

I thought he was joking at first, but he wasn't kidding around. He really liked the song because he liked to beat his wife and smoke and drink a lot.

I don't think he understood the irony.

That should have been a warning.

LEAVING THE TEMPLE

We stayed the night at Geneva and Hope's apartment. They weren't regular dancers who traveled on a regional circuit or anything. They were just hometown girls — albeit attractive ones — who danced for the money and the attention.

The next morning was Sunday, and I planned to attend mass at St. John's Church. Father Pontiac had invited me the previous night. Hope stayed in bed, and Richard and Geneva went out for breakfast. Steve and Mr. U. came with me. I was really surprised when they decided to go, but it made me feel good, like I was part of their band.

To be quite honest, I hadn't been a regular at church for some time. I sat on the wooden pew at St. John's and gazed upon all the suffering depicted in the statues, paintings, and stained glass.

That was odd.

You'd think all the nails and blood and tears would put a damper on what Father Pontiac called "a celebration." But I guess this was church, and everybody expected suffering.

From the very start of the services, I noticed all was not right with Father Pontiac.

His hand gestures were awkward, and his speech was a little slurred. I think — and I really, really hate to say this — I think he was intoxicated, which was odd because he had only sipped on cans of Coke the night before at Pandora's Box.

No one else seemed to notice, so I didn't say anything. By the time he was to read the Bible and give a sermon, my former teacher appeared to be struggling with his balance. He accidentally bumped into the microphone, making a noise loud enough to raise Lazarus from the dead. Again.

"Sorry about that," he said, too loudly. The church crowd, who had all apparently been asleep, knee-jerked to attention and called in reverent response: "And also with you."

He tried to explain, "I guess that I stumbled there."

They gave a requisite response in unison.

"Thanks be to God!"

I felt like I was watching one of the old films — the early talkies, with the soundtrack, a separate entity from the feature film, out of sync with the pictures and making no sense. Father Pontiac did his best to call his congregation back to the reading, but he was tipsy, making the situation difficult and extremely sad to watch.

He could not read anything without his glasses. We all learned about that the very first day in his history class. Every day he would begin with his glasses perched on his nose while reading from his preordained lecture notes. And every day he would suddenly announce, "Well! I don't need these to talk about history." He would then put his glasses and notes down and tell us tales of high historical adventure, human triumph, and, of course, human folderol.

He was our blind Homer, the consummate storyteller, who conjured in our young brains the ways and times of the ancient world.

THE ENGLISH SETTER DANCE

He told us all about Rome, a great civilization gone a bit mad with the power of its own self-concept. We laughed at the stories about poor Christians left to the lions in the Coliseum. What did we know? We were just ninth-graders who knew nothing of the smell of death, or the color of blood when there is too much of it and it mixes with the dust in the air and dirt on the ground.

What did we know? We were just kids who had never heard the sound a man makes when his skin is torn from his body.

What did we know?

So Father Pontiac left teaching after fifteen years because all he could do was make us laugh. He was right about that. He did make us laugh. We all loved his class. But Father Pontiac told me that night at the strip joint that he had failed as a teacher because he could not make us understand the darkness and ruin in the deep catacombs of the human heart, which are perpetuated when one person, for the worship of power, forsakes human dignity and offers others' arms and legs and heads and, finally, their hearts at the altar of his own ego.

So he quit teaching because all he could do, ultimately, was make us laugh.

Father Pontiac's history was just a good story to us. I guess being a teacher is dangerous. I guess it's sad, too. But none of it was his fault.

What did we know?

Every new plant, every generation, must find out about the one mendacious vine which is always coiling, serpent-like, and desiring nothing more than to cut the lifeblood from its fellow vegetation. That sort of thing just can't be explained. It can't be taught. But, Father Pontiac, at least you tried. And for that you deserve some thanks.

I remember one day in class when Father read us a letter he had received from Greg LaPoint, a former student of some years and older brother to Gary, one of my classmates. The letter was not mean-spirited, but Cpl. Greg, writing from Vietnam, said he was shocked because the war in which he was mired was very different from the history stories and movies in Father's class.

He had laughed in class.

But he never laughed in Vietnam.

He admitted, yes, there had been tales of bloodshed and death, but they were nothing like the bloodshed and death in his real war. He said there wasn't even a soundtrack. There had been no music playing at all when he had watched his friend Jerry Evans—a buddy, a classmate, a person some of us knew—die in a firefight. He said there was so much blood from that fight that pools of it formed on the ground because dear Mother Earth had to pause and take a breath before she could absorb more of it.

He said there was so much screaming that he couldn't take it anymore and that he didn't know which was worse: the blood or the screams or the fact there was no music playing when Jerry died in his arms.

He said that he had cupped his hands to catch Jerry's blood and that he had tried to put it all back into the veins in Jerry's body. But the blood had become sticky and thick and dirty. It was impossible to put it all back.

It was just not possible.

And there was no music at all.

There was just sticky, thick, dirty blood all over everything.

He said Jerry's heart just kept pumping the dark red stuff out of his body. Greg said he had learned one thing in Vietnam, and it wasn't much. He had learned that there should always be music playing when a friend's heart pumps its last echo of life upon the foliage and footprints and gunpowder and viscous puddles of war.

Without music, Cpl. Greg wrote in his letter, the reality of death is just too awful.

And at that moment, he said, life wasn't worth the price of admission.

When Father Pontiac had finished reading the letter, I remember two kids in the back of the room laughed. They laughed because they thought the letter was just another one of good old Pontiac's stories. Father Pontiac just stared at the two of them after he read the letter.

He didn't say anything.

He didn't say anything at all.

But he never wore his plaid sports jacket ever again. He only wore regular sports jackets, like all the other teachers. They all had really wide lapels. Everyone wore coats with wide lapels in those days.

# # #

Father Pontiac removed his glasses while standing, slightly inebriated, in front of his parishioners that day at St. John's, ready to read from The Acts of the Apostles.

"This is a reading," he said slowly. "This is a reading from a letter from the Apostle Paul to the...to the...to the."

He paused, looking confused.

Without his glasses, Father Pontiac was in trouble.

"Well," he finally said, "it must have been to somebody, but I can't for the life of me remember who it was right now."

I desperately hoped he wouldn't launch into a story about Christians and hungry Roman lions.

He didn't.

Instead, he shifted gears and started talking about King Herod, which was good because we expected to hear something about the Bible and most of us knew Herod was an evil guy who did something terrible in some Bible story. He told us King Herod liked fancy clothes better than anything else, and the people in his kingdom suffered a lot because of his vanity.

Then two strangers came to his kingdom and said they could make him special magical clothes, the finest in any land. Of course, Herod wanted these clothes. The two men said these special clothes were magical because only people who had been good would be able to see them.

In truth, the men made no clothing at all.

They kept all the money given to them for the material and just pretended to stitch and sew.

No one in the kingdom, not even the friends of King Herod, would dare admit the truth, because to say the truth—to admit they saw no clothing—implied they were not good people. If they had been good, they should be able to see the beautiful garments being made.

Even Herod could not admit the truth, and he, too, pretended to marvel at the magical wardrobe being made just for him.

Ultimately, old King Herod ended up a foolish and

naked man because he just had to prove to everyone that he was, indeed, a good guy.

Then Father Pontiac, the man who could never really explain the sound a man made when his flesh was torn from his body, told all of us about the stripper he had watched the previous night.

He said her name was Hope.

He told us how she had allowed a man in a wheelchair — a man who had a saggy face and a humped back, a man who held a folded dollar in his hand — to touch her thigh, then her knee, and, finally, her naked calf.

Then Father Pontiac said, "I'm certainly not saying anyone should be a stripper. But, if you are one, at least be a kind one."

He paused in silence.

These were the words of Father Pontiac's Gospel.

A few people even said, "Amen."

The Mass ended, and Father did his best to bid us all farewell. He thanked me for coming to church. He didn't say anything about being drunk, but I knew he was sorry and maybe even embarrassed about it.

As we passed through the church door and left the temple, a well-dressed woman, probably a regular at the church, stopped the three of us and said in a stern voice, "You three didn't come dressed for God's Holy Communion, did you?"

"I didn't know this was a dinner date," Mr. U. said, sarcastically. He was wearing a pair of bell-bottomed jeans with an American flag sewn on the flared pant leg. "If I had known, I'd have worn my tux."

The woman pointed her finger and shook it at us.

"I bet you're hippies," she said. "You're hippies, aren't you? I didn't think hippies went to church. I thought you just smoked your Mother Nature and those Doobie Brothers."

Mr. U. just looked at the woman for a minute. "On second thought," he said, "my tux wouldn't be good enough. I think I would have just come naked.

"God would have liked that."

The woman didn't answer him. She just walked away.

I think that Mr. U. was probably right.

If we all attended church in the nude, we'd throw fewer stones.

It's not as easy to dwell on others' secrets when your own are full frontal to the world.

MEANWHILE

Steve began to smoke cigars as part of our show. He also wore T-shirts to make himself look tough. Then he pushed one of his own songs on the band. It was all instrumental. Steve could never write words. He just didn't have any words in him. Even after all these years, I still have to tell the truth about his song: it sounded just like "Iron Man" by Black Sabbath, except without lyrics.

Steve also told us all we had to be more aggressive on stage. Sometimes he would throw drinks at the audience or flick his cigar ashes at the girls on the dance floor.

He insisted that we play Richard's "I'm Not That Stupid To Be That Stupid" song. He changed his bass line in that song to a slow, heavy thud that, in my opinion, made a potentially humorous song into a scary one. It began to crawl like a nightmare on the prowl, and he sometimes joined Richard with the lead vocals of the song.

I remember more verses:

I see two old women with a flat tire,
Stranded on the side of the road,
I should stop, but radio's playin' a good tune,
And outside it's much too cold.

MEANWHILE

The world's my garbage can,
To dump my butts and ash.
And if you don't like it mister,
Then you can just kiss my trash.

When Richard sang the song by himself, the words were
funny and self-effacing, which is the way he wrote them.
That's the point of the song. Its title could mean we really
shouldn't be that stupid, or it could mean some people prefer
to be stupid because it enables them to live a carefree life.

When Steve screamed those same words, they became
a flagpole for selfish and mean people to raise a symbol of
their stupidity.

Did he know what he was doing?

I think so, but he got all caught up in the fact that several
regulars kept coming to our shows and making a big deal
about the song and his performance. They egged him on,
and he liked the attention so much he probably did things
he shouldn't or wouldn't have considered if his fans were
not present.

He even shaved his head, which was a strange thing to
do in 1974.

The regulars, our supposed fans, loved his haircut.

One of the regulars was the guy from Pandora's Box
who so identified with the song. He was the guy who liked
to beat his wife and smoke in front of his kids.

After a time, Steve's fans shaved their heads, too. I
watched as Steve took his cigar and shoved it into Lola's
mouth during one performance of the song. She thought
it was a dog treat, until it made her cough and spit up on
the stage. Steve's fan club cheered and held up their fists

in approval.

They all laughed.

But it made me mad.

He had hurt Lola.

For most of the show, I have to admit, Steve did hold his own. He really was a great bass player who made the band sound good. He was also a friend, so Richard looked the other way quite a bit. I recall one exchange between them during which I knew Richard was very angry. Steve had shown up with his customary tight T-shirt, but had marked it up with a black swastika.

His loyal fan club followed their leader—the guy who beat his wife—and I watched as they goose-stepped to our version of "I Heard It Through the Grapevine."

How ironic. I wonder if Hitler would have approved of the song?

But that didn't concern them. It was all just a bit of fun and, to them, having fun was going way too far.

After the performance, I heard Richard admonish Steve.

"No more of that swastika stuff. It's stupid."

Steve said he didn't understand because it was all part of the act.

Richard pointed his finger in Steve's face.

I had never seen him do that before.

"I said knock off the Nazi stuff!" he shouted.

I heard him say that.

His finger gouged the flesh under Steve's eye.

Steve backed off.

"Sure," he said. "OK."

But I saw an angry look in his eyes, especially the one with the red mark underneath it.

Later in life, I saw this look again. A man who had long since stopped loving—or even liking—his wife had that look when he twisted a cruel word like a knife to hurt the one woman he once claimed to love. The love was long gone, and all that remained was the urge to inflict pain, and this made their marriage worthwhile.

So our band continued to play music. We became that marriage.

Steve's eyes gave notice that he wanted to get even. He had backed off and tried to be Richard's friend again, his pal. He simply pretended to be a friend, and for all the wrong reasons.

Molly sang well.

She even managed to dance a little during a couple of the songs.

I know it bothered her when Geneva and Hope began to show up when we played. Sometimes, I could catch her eyes as she sang. She would look into the audience—scanning— for Richard's new and sudden girlfriend.

Oddly enough, she sang better when the two girls were on the floor dancing. Was it out of anger? Maybe. Or was it out of passion? Was it out of competition with a world that would not, or could not, or was not able to give her what she wanted?

I really can't say for sure.

Why Geneva? Why did Richard want to be with her of all people?

At first I thought maybe Richard spent his time with her because he saw a song in her. But now, after thinking about this for years, I believe her appeal was just the opposite. Richard knew there was absolutely no song whatsoever in

Geneva. Her heart held no secret words for anyone to find. And this fascinated our Richard.

It might have even been a necessary respite for him.

I remember one of the very last times Molly sang with us in public. She was all dressed up and looked really beautiful in a long peasant skirt that was red and gold—in a stained glass window design. She wore green leather boots. I watched as she sang the lead vocal on Steve's slow dance choice, "I Don't Know How to Love Him."

I watched her eyes as she caught sight of Geneva at a table toward the back of the bar. As Molly sang, I watched Geneva's lips move in silent victory. Together, they reminded me of those two masks of good theater, the happy comic and the sad tragedian: the first content with the whims of romance, and the other doomed to possess forever the empty heart.

That was the night Molly made my eyes tear with her voice.

After our show, Richard and Geneva walked toward the door. Their backs were turned to the rest of us in the bar. All alone, Molly stood by the stage and watched as they left.

I looked at Molly.

It was the moment I knew I no longer felt something toward her just because she was so beautiful. My heart didn't pound because she sang such a lovely song. Instead, I wanted to be near her because I felt an odd combustion of compassion, sadness, and a strange gravitational sensation, a gravity pulling me closer to what she wanted and what she needed. I longed to hold all the loneliness she held in her heart.

Molly had secret words waiting to be found, and I

wanted to know those words. I wanted to make those words into the lyrics of a song.

It's easy to love someone who is happy and strong, but my love for Molly was different. All the cards were on the table, and I realized I wasn't the King of Hearts, and there was nothing I could do to fix the deck and deal her the card she so desperately wanted to hold in her hand.

This feeling called love made me feel old and helpless.

"Sorry," I said.

"You noticed."

"It's pretty obvious."

She shook her head.

"No. That's not what I meant. I meant that you noticed me.

"Every young girl learns eventually that she will never be pretty enough for this universe." She smiled and swayed her body and our shoulders touched. "But you noticed."

We walked out of the bar together.

Soon after that, I wrote my one bit of rock and roll lyricism.

A stone of inspiration struck me, and I wrote the words to "Branches Unseen," which was all about Molly. Of course, it never mentioned her name. I was much too shy for that sort of thing. The actual words were about some evergreens in the woods around our cabin. The cedars were growing so close to each other that the very bottom branches, the ones hiding there, were being shaded out by the new growth, which was very lush and very green because it was taking all the sunshine.

The words, though, weren't only about Molly. It occurred to me that so many things—so many common people, so many common places — are often shaded out and left unnoticed. It's really a shame. My words were about finding out it was too late to tell someone or something how much they meant.

When Steve read the words, he liked them enough to graft them onto his "Iron Man" sound-a-like instrumental he had forced the band to play. They didn't fit his music at all, but that was all right at the time because I thought it was great to have written half of a song.

We called it "Our Tree Song."

That's what the title read on the flip side of our one big song we recorded as a single. It's my one little contribution to the history of rock music: I wrote the lyrics to the B-side of our local flop single.

No one really cares, but even after all these years, I know the song isn't just about cedar trees. And although her name is never mentioned, the song is really about Molly and the night when she watched as Richard and Geneva left together after our show.

Meanwhile, Mr. U. found something new in a stack of old rhythm and blues records someone donated to a local St. Vincent DePaul store. He persuaded the rest of us to play a few Willie Dixon songs to which Steve's idiot fan club continued to do their goose-step dance. I can think of about six million good reasons why they shouldn't have pretended to be disciples of Hitler.

That night, Mr. U. broke a drumstick. He was so furious at the stupidity of those fools.

Perhaps a week or two after Steve's swastika performance, Mr. U.'s anger caused him more trouble. Steve's fan club had swelled to about twenty-five guys and a few of their girlfriends. They all knew our song, "I'm Not That Stupid To Be That Stupid." They liked the song a lot, but for all the wrong reasons.

The fans were loud and made a big deal of our show. Mr. U. kept saying that if the big labels heard about the excitement, we might get signed to a record deal. He really did, more than any of us, want to make a record.

So he tolerated some of the stuff he didn't like very much.

We were playing in Sheboygan that night. About thirty of the fans were there. More seemed to show up every time we played. We were taking a break between sets when four or five of the fans grabbed Molly. One even put his arm around her. They sang the line from our "Stupid Song" about "fighting for any pretty girl's right to be a centerfold in Playboy." All the while they eyed her lustfully.

"This one could be in my Playboy!" the guy with his arm around her said. He gave Molly a tight squeeze.

Another one put his arm around her and said, "What do you think, honey? You and me and a Polaroid. I won't even charge for the session. What do you say?"

He spilled some of his drink on our Molly.

Then I saw our drummer, all five foot ten and a half, one hundred and fifty pounds of him, including his down-to-the-waist hair, step up to the guys as they surrounded our Molly.

He wasn't laughing.

Mr. U. took a step closer to them, and one of the fans put his hand on the drummer's shoulder.

The guy's hand stroked his long hair.

Then the fan stiffened his arm and tried to push our

drummer to the side.

Mr. U. easily batted his hand away.

"Leave her alone," he said.

"Sure," one of them said, and they took another step back. "Sure. No problem. But I'll tell you, you just keep being the drummer and play your music. Dance with your dog. We're just here for a good time.

"Here, pal. Have a cigarette."

Mr. U. didn't smoke.

They walked away. I took a deep breath—the first in several minutes.

We thought it was over.

We were wrong.

After the show, when Molly and I went to put our gear away in the back of Mr. U.'s TUG-mobile van, we found three of its tires had been slashed to ribbons.

"Why did they leave one tire?" I asked, not believing the violence.

"It's just their idea of a joke," Molly said.

"I don't get it."

"Well," she said, "ask Steve. He might understand. He'd think it was funny." Bitterness crept into her voice. "Or ask Richie. He wrote that stupid song."

I looked at her eyes, and I knew she really didn't want to sing in our little band anymore. The summer night suddenly turned cold, and every star in the sky was dim and distant.

We continued to play shows. Molly continued to sing the songs. More people continued to show up. And, of course, Richard continued to sing about The Revolution and leaving the temple.

MEANWHILE

I didn't believe him anymore.

I knew Molly had given up, and it wasn't just because of Geneva and her constant presence at every show. It was more than that—much more.

We still played the music we loved. That had been the whole point of the band. We even had a popular song. But everything had gone wrong because people loved the song for all the wrong reasons. Our fans, they were just lunatics who pulled the strings. Those lunatics had the keys to the asylum doors, and I know now that those doors should have remained locked.

So Molly wanted out, and I know Geneva was pushing Richard to let her sing in the band. She and Hope still sat in the back and watched while we played, but I knew that Geneva would leave Hope behind in a flash to sip drinks by herself so she could be the singing star on stage.

That's just the way she was, and that was a shame because Hope deserved more from a friend.

I honestly didn't know what to make of Richard anymore.

I know Steve was his old friend. So I know he let Steve's foolishness go, although they did have that one big fight over the Nazi dance. Richard kept playing, and he should have stopped. His "Stupid Song" just became longer and longer. I suppose the song's subject matter, the insanity of the human race, is an endless highway, which we all sweat to build, and we fight to drive on, until we all run out of gas or just cough ourselves to death. The freeway of human stupidity is, indeed, a long and awfully winding road.

That was exactly the problem: the more Richard sang the song and the more people thought the song was humorous, the greater the urge was to write yet another verse. Maybe he hoped if he sang enough silly rhymes about how dumb we can all be, then someday, finally, the crowds would get the message, and then they would stop laughing long enough to be decent spouses, or think about hungry kids with big bellies, or care a little bit and help others who are stranded by the side of the road.

But we played on.

Of course we played on.

That's all we could do.

We were a rock 'n' roll band, and we were becoming famous. Fifty or sixty fans would show up and sing the song. They were our fans. They would eagerly applaud the old verses about pizza and beer in the fridge, and then they would wait, starry-eyed, for new words, which Richard would sometimes make up on the spot.

He seemed to enjoy the irony. He enjoyed the joke on the fans.

One night he sang:

I didn't bother to vote for president,
And I don't know what freedom is for.
But my stupid kid finally found himself a job,
Killing Vietcong in the Vietnam War.

At that point, one of the fans jumped up like he just won the big payoff at Friday night bingo. He danced around like a madman and ripped off his shirt. Underneath he wore a T-shirt. The shirt had originally read NO NUKES! This was a reasonable thing to say on a T-shirt. The fan had crossed the NUKES part of the message and had changed the words

MEANWHILE

so the shirt now read NO GOOKS!
    That was a cruel thing to say on a shirt.
    We all saw the shirt at the same time.
    Steve laughed.
    Molly stopped singing.
    God! I truly wish Richard had stopped that night.

THIS IS EVENTUALLY

Making our one bit of rock and roll history — The English Setter Dance's only attempt at a bona-fide hit single — took a lot longer than the actual playing time of the song, which only required two minutes and thirty-one seconds of radio air space.

It was our sometime manager, Rock 'n' Roll Randy, who brought us the big news. Rock 'n' Roll Randy, God bless him, had traded a copy of the very first Magna Carta album, the Holy Grail of folk rock music, to a certain Mr. Randal Heckle in exchange for real studio time. It was exactly what we needed to record our little bit of history.

This is a great opportunity to point out what a rock 'n' roll saint of a guy our Randy was to the band. Sure, he only spoke in rock band titles and songs, but that was completely understandable from a guy whose heart pounded incessantly to the drumbeat of great rock songs. Yes, he did have a rock 'n' roll heart. He even traded his precious album to get his band, his English Setter Dance, into a studio for one chance at big-time music immortality.

What a guy.

Later in life, as I sat copying my thoughts onto paper for these memoirs, I thought it was important to track down a copy of our band's record. I wanted to play it while I was writing this book. I also thought it would be a nice wedding gift for Carrie Hogey, the sister of Buzz and Kevin. You'll recall that her birth control pills were the placebo drugs that caused all the problems for Junior Weston, the former football star who held a personal vendetta against yours truly.

When it was recorded, our single sold zilch, and I thought that Rock 'n' Roll Randy would certainly have all the unsold copies. I found him at Brown County Social Services Hospital, formerly known as Brown County Mental Hospital, so... well, you probably get the picture. I had not seen Randy in some twenty-five years. Yet when he noticed me in the visitors' area, he waved.

What a guy.

He and his fellow hospital friends were actively involved in a game of Trivial Pursuit, the baby-boomers rock music edition. Randy's team was winning. He wore a T-shirt that said, HARD ROCK CAFÉ ALPHA CENTAURI. Apparently, the franchise had, like our universe, expanded quite a bit.

The nurse took me aside and gave me a kind of warning. "Randy," she said as she shook her head, "can't really communicate." The nurse paused. "But I suppose you know that already because you're his friend."

I acted the innocent. "What do you mean?"

"Well," she whispered, "he never makes any sense."

She shook her head slowly.

"He goes on and on about Floyd's pink tangerines and Jethro's atomic roosters. He seems to like some place called Emerson Lake."

The nurse touched her temple with one finger and leaned closer to me.

"He says he's a stooge at a funhouse and he keeps telling everyone that a King called Crimson rules."

I laughed.

The world made sense to me.

That doesn't happen very often. Ironically, this lucid moment was found in the confines of a mental hospital. Leave it to Rock 'n' Roll Randy.

What a guy.

So I prepared for the worst. Well, I was quite ready to shake my head knowingly and listen kindly to Randy's stream of rock band consciousness and album titles while trying to find some way to talk about our old lost 45.

"Van Morrison," Rock 'n' Roll Randy said as he shook my hand. "Van the man, you know."

I smiled and said, "Sure."

Randy smiled.

The nurse smiled.

"That's correct," a voice at the game table said. "Van Morrison sang 'Brown-Eyed Girl.' Randy, you're correct again."

"I wish they'd call me 'Rock 'n' Roll,'" Randy said. "And I wish they would start asking the tough questions."

I was shocked. I had just, for the first time, understood what Rock 'n' Roll said.

The nurse smiled sympathetically at me, "See what I mean?

"No, Randy," she said slowly. "This isn't Mr. Morrison. This is your friend, Peter Barooke. You remember him, don't you?" Apparently, she didn't understand.

"The people in control of everything are a bunch of idiots," Randy whispered.

I was amazed. This was a moment of afflatus. I finally understood every word he said. I had truly entered his world of rock music.

"The worst part," he said, "is that they don't even know they're a bunch of idiots."

I was still amazed.

The nurse continued to smile.

Randy pulled me closer and whispered in a secretive voice, "They all think that I'm Elvis Presley."

"They do?" I tried to be polite.

"Sure.

"I know all the answers in the trivia game."

"I can understand that."

"But I'm not Elvis, though," he said.

"That's good." I was relieved.

"Oh no." Randy leaned toward me and pointed his finger. "That guy over there is." He laughed to himself. "But don't tell anybody. You know Elvis. He doesn't want to be recognized. So he's in disguise."

"Disguise?"

"Yeah. They all think he's Buddy Holly." Randy leaned even closer. "But he isn't Buddy Holly."

"Why not?" I asked.

He smiled and said, "Because that's who I really am. How else would I know all these answers to the trivia game?"

I didn't get any copies of our single from Rock 'n' Roll Randy that night. But it was really great to see such a true-hearted player in the game of rock trivia. Randy's problem was he lived for things that just didn't matter to most people. But those things mattered a lot to him. They probably mattered too much.

Well, Randy, thanks for caring about our band and our music. You loved it more than we did. You are rock 'n' roll. And I finally understand everything you said.

As we gathered at Heckle Studio that night, we were a little loose at the seams, and quite a bit of the stuffing was falling out of the band. For a group who was about to enter the portals or rock 'n' roll Heaven, we were having an awfully tough time getting through the eye of the needle.

Molly didn't want to be there anymore.

Steve insisted his instrumental, with my "Tree Song" lyrics, had to be on the flip side of our single.

Mr. U. had never been this close to recording, so he was just plain nervous and a little edgy.

Richard had told Geneva she could sing on the record, but he didn't know how to tell the rest of us, especially Molly.

Only Randy experienced Nirvana. He found the sort of bliss that arrives only when dreams become three-dimensional reality long enough to shake your hand and offer the invite to a cup of coffee.

"Deep Purple," Randy said. "Warhorse and Captain Beyond. You know. *Machine Head.* 'Space Truckin'.' 'Maybe I'm a Leo.'"

He knew the importance of this moment. It was the band's moment. It was our music's moment. It was even a moment for dear Mrs. Clearwater. I watched as he prepared to make our record. His entire body shook.

Most importantly, this was his moment.

Years later, I was surprised that I couldn't find a copy of our band's single at our local junk shop, This Is Eventually. I was surprised because the place had everything nobody wanted at one time or another. The guy who owned the shop was Crazy Carl Carlson, and he had everything that didn't sell itself to the open arms of consumer whim.

Our one flop single certainly qualified for a place in his shop.

Our record sold less than a Lori Partridge solo album. Nobody wanted our song back in 1974, and except for Carrie's desire to sip the nascent waters of her youth and my hope for a unique wedding gift, nobody wanted it today.

That's why I was so surprised.

Crazy Carl apologized but said, "Don't worry. It'll show up here." He then tried to sell me a T-shirt that read: DEAR VISITING ALIENS! PLEASE DO NOT FEED THE HUMANS! SOME OF THEM ARE DANGEROUS AND CAN BE REALLY MEAN! Of course, I bought one.

I also found a copy of the one and only album by that weed guy's progressive rock band with so many different names. They never did become famous. The title of their album was *Trust Us: You Really Don't Want This Record.*

I remembered that night the drunken driver's car got caught on the spring.

The band finally recorded under the name Foghat Cancelled. Their name and title were stenciled in black gothic letters on a plain white cover.

I only paid two dollars for the album, but it's worth a lot more in Japan. They like old progressive rock records there. Once I watched a hardcore Japanese record collector eagerly sift his way through hard-to-find albums at a record fair. He wore white gloves to show pristine respect for the vinyl he gently held in his hands. I thought about Rock 'n' Roll Randy as I watched him inspect his treasures.

As I paid for the T-shirt and the album, I suddenly noticed that Carl's dog, Duchess, was markedly absent from the store. Her unoccupied bed rested on the floor beside Carl's rocking chair. Duchess was an Irish setter who had grown old and thin. Carl called her Duchy Gray Muzzle. Sadly, Crazy Carl told me, his Duchy had died. He had not yet found another dog to replace her in his heart.

That happens.

I know.

When Carl handed me the change, he pointed to a box with the sign: PLEASE DONATE YOUR SPARE CHANGE FOR YOUR FRIENDS AT THE ANIMAL SHELTER. I stood there for a moment and imagined new shoppers, when given this option, hesitating while Crazy Carl watched, almost like he was witnessing the great moment when their eternal salvation was decided.

I threw my change in the box.

Maybe Heaven can be obtained just by being kind to other creatures on our planet, but that almost seems too easy.

So I didn't have a copy of our single to give to Carrie Hogey as a present. I went to her wedding anyway. I went for old times' sake. I wanted to wish her well. I wanted to tell her good luck.

Ironically, she wasn't the one who needed the luck. Carrie married a guy named Raymond Luffy, brother to Norma Rose Luffy, who was cousin to many people, one of whom just happened to be Junior Weston, the bane of my teenaged life. Junior Weston was a tuxedoed part of the rather large wedding party.

As I stood in the reception line, I experienced the balm

of apparent reprieve, thinking about that moment at the Snickers candy bar machine when Junior failed to recognize me. My salvation was almost worth the Payday I was forced to eat.

Of course, I was wrong.

There was no escape this time.

As I shook his hand in the reception line, Junior grabbed me and pulled me close.

He smiled and said, "Hey, cross-country guy. I know who you are."

He squeezed my hand until the bones began to crack.

"I'm still going to hurt you because you caught that football," he whispered.

I just didn't feel like dancing with the bride after that.

Buzz Hogey, who was also a member of the wedding party, came to my rescue. He had plundered his sister's purse and had taken several quarters and her super-strength Prozac pills. While in the bathroom, he tried to pass these pills off as big-time drugs to various guests.

Old habits die hard, I guess.

Various ex-football stars from high school, including Junior Weston, met in the bathroom and decided to indulge themselves. Buzz eagerly produced his stash. At the last moment, one of the ex-footballers hesitated and suddenly said, "Hey Buzzy! These aren't your sister's birth control pills again, are they?"

Buzz assured him that the pills were not any form of contraceptive.

All the football heroes smiled. Then they yielded to the temptation of sister Carrie's Prozac.

It was a very good thing because later in the evening,

Junior confronted me about the big game-winning catch in that eighth grade football game.

He shook my hand in an extremely relaxed manner. He had considerably mellowed while under the chemical influence of Prozac.

"Hey. Cross-country guy," he said. "You know. That was a good catch. I'm not too angry anymore. I don't know why. But I'm just not feeling angry about the whole thing."

He smiled.

"I'm just not the kind of guy who holds a grudge."

It was the Prozac speaking because then he told me that for one hundred dollars he would forget the whole thing.

"Do you take MasterCard?" I asked.

He did!

Later in the evening, I approached Father Steve, the priest who had consecrated the wedding mass.

I told Father Steve I intended to light a votive thanksgiving candle.

"And why?" he asked. "Do you want to thank God?"

"For antidepressant drugs and MasterCard, father," I said.

"Well," he answered, "God works in wondrous and mysterious ways."

I had to agree.

He said, "Amen."

I said, "Amen."

He nodded his head knowingly and slowly walked away.

# # #

Molly didn't want to sing our song, "I'm Not That Stupid To Be That Stupid."

THIS IS EVENTUALLY

Molly didn't want to sing on anything we recorded that night.

That was a problem because even if Richard sang the lead vocal, our sound was the complement of male and female voices.

Not unexpectedly, Geneva grabbed at her chance to sing with our band. I strummed along as best I could on the first take of the recording, which wasn't very good. For the very last verse, Richard sang:

Sure. I'm not that stupid to be that stupid
And no one's worth befriending,
So enjoy the joke, and keep on laughing,
Right through to its sad and lonely ending.

We tried to record a second version, and I watched as Molly removed her headphones and slowly walked out of the recording area. Her eyes were red and watery.

I called her back and convinced her to do another take.

At first, she sang into the same microphone as Geneva. Then Geneva backed away because it was obvious who should be singing on the band's big recording.

Molly's voice was so beautiful and so sad, and that was part of the song's substance. It wasn't just a stupid song about people who don't care about anything. It was also a song about love and compassion and kindness.

I think Geneva discovered that, and that's why she backed further away from the microphone.

I watched her for a moment.

Then I, too, walked away. My guitar added absolutely nothing to the song.

THE ENGLISH SETTER DANCE

I was some distance from the band when I sensed Geneva standing next to me. We stood there by ourselves and watched The English Setter Dance collect itself together, possibly for the last time, to play a decent rock song, recorded that night for the universe to hear.

In those two minutes and thirty-one seconds, everything I have come to love about rock music existed so clearly, for the very first time, right before my eyes. Rock 'n' roll gave smart people a chance to be not so smart, and it gave not-so-smart people a chance to be clever. It gave the body a chance to celebrate the heart, and it gave the heart a chance to celebrate the body. Sadness harmonized with happiness. The genteel hand softly touched the profane word. The sagacious old man finally laughed at the jester's dirty joke.

Or something like that.

When they had finished recording their song—when they had finished their bit of eternity—Rock 'n' Roll Randy yelled, "Zappa, man. *Hot Rats. Burnt Weeny Sandwich. Lumpy Gravy. Absolutely Free. Cruising with Ruben and the Jets.*"

I could not translate his exact words, but I was beginning to understand his rock 'n' roll world.

Molly stood by my side. I saw the tears in her eyes.

"That's it," she said. "I can't sing like this anymore."

She was right.

Maybe her imagination had caught a glimpse of the future.

She couldn't sing like this without some secret sense, some secret intuition. Her heart was just too young to know such sadness any other way.

EVEN GOD WAITS FOR HIS PIZZA TONIGHT

As Rock 'n' Roll Randy arrived at the cabin, he only said one word: "Rockin'."

I had no idea what he meant.

Everyone else apparently did, except Geneva, who was our new singer because Molly had just left the group.

Richard and Mr. U. looked at each other. Then Richard strummed a few "American Woman" chords on his guitar.

"The Guess Who! They're playing here!" Mr. U. shouted.

Randy unfolded a concert poster and smiled.

Richard's eyes became very blue.

He was seldom excited, but this was news! The Guess Who, Richard's all time favorite band, was playing in Green Bay. They were, according to the poster, to be supported by special guests Foghat and a local group known as GegGeg Nug. It was going to be a big show.

We all loved The Guess Who. We listened to their records all the time. In 1974, they were one of the biggest touring bands in America, especially in our midwest America. Their lead singer, Burton Cummings, the voice that sang all those hits, was a magical performer. He always put on quite a show. What a voice.

Their guitarist was Kurt "The Walrus" Winter. "The Walrus" was the everyman guitar hero who managed to rock the world just a little bit.

That was important in 1974. I think it's still important today.

We all loved Kurt Winter. He wore the same clothes every day. Every photo of "The Walrus" showed him wearing the same sweatshirt. It was gray and sleeveless, and it carried the logo: SOUND BY GARNET: WINNIPEG, CANADA.

We loved Kurt because he was really just one of us—nothing more, and certainly nothing less. Yet "The Walrus" trod the stage floorboards as a bona-fide rock star. He trod those floorboards with the same clothes every day.

You see, for some of us, clothes really didn't matter all that much. Music mattered. Ideas mattered. It mattered if the world was rocked just a little bit. So this concert was really a big deal. The Guess Who was a great rock band, and they were playing in Green Bay.

We had tickets. We had tickets to feel the world being rocked. We had tickets to transport us through the mirror into a world of Burton Cummings' voice and Kurt "The Walrus" Winter's guitar playing. We had tickets into a magical world where music and song lyrics mattered more than anything else.

Rock 'n' Roll Randy had been right when he said that one word.

He had only said, "Rockin'."

And everybody understood.

Richard was really excited on the day of the show. I had

never seen him like that. I was accustomed to seeing him on stage playing "Thanks, Mrs. Clearwater" or "Onward, Christian Canines." For the first time, I saw my hero as a star-struck fan. That's what he was. Maybe that's what we all are. We're all just fans, one way or another.

I was Richard's number one fan. I admit it. I idolized him because of all the songs he sang. Yet he was in awe of Burton Cummings and The Guess Who. He was their fan. He hummed all their melodies, and he sang all their words.

I still remember the look in Richard's eyes on the night of the concert. It was an odd combination of reverence and predation. Adam and Eve probably had a similar look as they were about to eat that apple. It was a glance revealing an appetite for sweet innocence as it still lingered on the tart taste buds of humanity.

I had seen the look once before while I was in high school. I saw the look on the very day Junior Weston asked me to sign his petition to allow him to play in the next football game, even though he had violated the school drug code by swallowing Buzz Hogey's sister's birth control pills, thinking that they were big-time drugs.

I had just bought a Payday candy bar. I wanted a Snickers, but I had panicked when Junior surprised me, so I pulled the wrong candy bar knob and had to settle for a Payday.

Earlier on that same day, I found a notebook left on my third period math class desk. It was a red notebook, and I knew exactly who owned it. Everyone knew the guy. Well, we didn't know his real name. We just called him The Monk. The Monk had mysteriously joined our class several months into the year. He came out of no particular place, and looked like a Marine. But he wasn't a Marine.

EVEN GOD WAITS FOR HIS PIZZA TONIGHT

He always carried a Bible. He never really talked to anyone. He always read his Bible. He also had comic books with him. At the time, I thought comic books and the Bible were a strange combination, but now I'm not quite so certain about anything like that.

The Monk's complexion was Moby Dick white. I suppose we should have called him Ahab, but we were not yet clever enough in life to do that.

So we just called him The Monk.

I knew it was his red notebook because I had watched him write in it during my sixth hour social studies class. That's all he ever did. He just wrote his thoughts in that notebook. The teachers, I suppose, thought he was diligently taking notes. But he wasn't even listening to their lecture. He was in a world of his own, somewhere quite far from the confines of High School, USA.

He was odd, and he was very quiet.

So we called him The Monk just like Kurt Winter was called "The Walrus," and we watched as he wrote in that notebook every hour of every day.

Then he left his notebook in math class, and I found it. Boy! Did I want to read his every word! This guy was a real high school mystery. I had the key. I had his notebook. I opened the front cover. The opening page read:

Please don't read this without permission. It contains the private thoughts of someone who wants to keep his thoughts hidden from the world. So please, return this notebook to its owner. You know who I am. Everyone calls me The Monk. I'm sure you have called me that, too. You know who I am.

Thanks for being a decent human being!

I didn't know what to do.

I really did want to invade his privacy and read everything he wrote in the notebook, yet there was a strange earnestness in his request. It was a plea for honesty and decency and maturity, all odd things to a high school student who was used to cheering for football teams and football cheerleaders at pep rallies. After a thousand missteps and almost peeks, I did the unthinkable: I returned the notebook, unopened and unread, to its original owner.

I didn't do it out of guilt.

I did it because it seemed at the time to be the right thing to do.

The Monk just smiled when I gave him his notebook. That's where I saw the very same look I had seen in Richard when we went to see The Guess Who. The Monk's eyes were like that all the time, I suppose, but this was the moment I noticed. He was showing his gratitude.

That was the very first time I had ever glimpsed into the eyes of someone who knew a bit more about the universe than the average human being, which may be as much a prayer as it is a profanation. Everything in our universe may be nothing more than a coin flip.

The Monk was really quite free from the everyday worries bothering the rest of us. He wrote about things I really did not know. His eyes trusted me. I could have been lying to him. I might have read his notebook before I gave it back. That thought never occurred to him. He just took me at my word and was genuinely pleased I had honored his request.

Then The Monk looked beyond me, over my shoulder, at the long lines of eager and impatient students, who, with money in hand, were waiting to buy their favorite food from the vending machines in our school's cafeteria.

"Do you ever think," he suddenly asked in a friendly tone, "that we eat too much junk food?"

I looked at the Payday candy bar in my hand.

I didn't give him an answer.

"I was just thinking," he said thoughtfully. "If everyone eats these Twinkies and fat-saturated potato chips and, well, whatever is in those machines, we'll eventually evolve into a species thriving on junk food. You know what I mean?"

He paused.

"It will be the survival of the fittest. Those who will live a long time while eating all that junk food will eventually populate the earth with their offspring whose bodies will like that stuff. They will crave it. They'll need all the salt and grease and sugar. They'll even need tar from cigarettes.

"It will all be health food then because everyone who can't stand the stuff will die off from clogged arteries and lung cancer."

I looked at my Payday candy bar again.

"It will be the survival of the fattest," I suggested.

The Monk laughed quietly.

"Someday," he pointed to my candy bar. "Someday that stuff will be sold in health food stores everywhere."

"It will be right next to the potato chips, garlic pretzel mix, and cheese-flavored popcorn," I said. "That sounds great."

"Well," The Monk said. "Don't get your hopes up. It'll take a long time. And it's just a thought, you know. It's just an idea. But it's sort of interesting to think if junk food becomes the survival diet—you know, if it becomes the good stuff—what will be the junk food?

"Maybe all the vegetables and fruits and grains nobody wants to eat today will be the bad stuff of tomorrow. Can you imagine?" He paused and pointed to the long lines of still impatient students standing at the vending machines. "Can you imagine those kids standing there to buy a small bag of asparagus, or cauliflower, or mixed dried fruit?"

"And they'll want to eat that healthy stuff?" I asked.

"Sure. It's all a big circle. Everything's a circle. By then it will be the bad stuff, the forbidden fruit. That's what we all want, especially the kids. We always want the forbidden stuff. Look at Adam and Eve. They were drooling over an apple while some snake told them it was all right to take a bite."

"Wow." I looked at my Payday candy bar. "I guess I should have pulled a knob for an apple."

The Monk smiled. "Maybe the devil should have talked Eve into a Payday candy bar. Who knows? When everything comes full circle, the apple will be illicit pleasure again."

"Then," I suggested, "then we would all be back in the Garden of Eden."

The Monk was silent.

"Do you think we'd all be better off?" I asked.

"I doubt it," he said. "It probably wouldn't make much of a difference. I don't think anything makes much of a difference. You know. Nothing is all that important. Apples are about the same as a candy bar."

I had to agree.

Then I said, "Maybe Eve never really wanted that apple. Maybe she didn't want that forbidden fruit. Maybe she just wanted an orange or some apricot. Maybe the snake just scared her, and she grabbed that apple by mistake.

"That happens sometimes," I said as I took another bite of my Payday.

The Monk nodded slowly.

I pointed to his Bible and stack of comic books. "Maybe we've got it all wrong. Maybe the whole thing isn't really based on any kind of evil. Maybe the whole thing just happened because of panic and a whole lot of fear. Maybe Eve just pulled the wrong knob on the fruit vending machine."

"Could be," he smiled. "But that was one hell of a wrong pull on the wrong vending machine knob."

Again, I had to agree. Perhaps life is nothing more than a pull on a vending machine knob.

I liked The Monk. I was glad I had not read his notebook. Unfortunately, I never talked with him again. He never graduated with our class. He slipped away as silently as he had entered our school. But I remember that look in his eyes. It was the very same look I saw in Richard as he stood in line and waited to see his favorite rock band perform his favorite songs. He still had a tart appetite for the sweetness of innocence.

The first band playing was called GegGeg Nug. They were a local group. The band was named after its lead singer. We all knew her. GegGeg Nug wasn't her real name. She was really Tammy Leonot, and her father was an alcoholic. She just called herself GegGeg Nug and claimed to be an exchange student from Edina, which was a planet somewhere in the universe. Nobody was quite sure about its exact location. We just knew it didn't have a Hard Rock Café, which was a bit surprising. We knew her father drank booze all the time and she was an alien exchange student from Edina. That was all we ever really needed to know.

It was really all that mattered.

GegGeg Nug's brother wasn't an exchange student from another planet, but he did claim to have been abducted by aliens who wanted to know more about the human race. His story was a great pick up line.

I suppose he left a lot to the imagination.

As GegGeg Nug prepared to play their music, I noticed two things. First, they set their equipment up on the floor of the arena, rather than on the stage. Then I noticed their guitarist was Jonathan Maenad, the brother to Sylvie Maenad, whose party I attended on the night of my high school graduation. They were a punk band. Their sweat dripped into the beer of the dance floor. They were a punk band long before The Ramones or The Sex Pistols. I suppose that made them special in an Iggy and the Stooges sort of way.

GegGeg came on the floor and informed us all that the show was running really late and the promoters said they could only play for fifteen minutes. For them, this meant they could only play twenty songs. All the fans of The Guess Who were really impatient and didn't want to listen to any opening act—although, when the band refused to play on stage, a few people seemed to warm to them.

They liked GegGeg's short leather skirt. Their final song was written by Jonathan Maenad. It was called "Serfing USA." We all clapped because we thought it was a cover of The Beach Boys' song. But we were wrong. It had nothing to do with surfing the waves. I remember GegGeg singing:

Pay for that car with your life,
Get everything you want to get,

EVEN GOD WAITS FOR HIS PIZZA TONIGHT

And watch the banker and the business man
Take your freedom with your debt.
We all just wanted to surf the waves,
And watch girls on sandy beaches,
But now we're drowning in our debt,
And we're sucked to death by leeches.
Serfing, USA.
I paid with credit today.
Serfing USA,
I just sold my freedom away.

I guess they had a point. Of course, it was just a punk rock point. Sure, we all have sold ourselves. We've sold our freedom, and we have begged for credit from big business because we want to buy stuff we can't afford. Sure, we work crappy jobs because we owe money to people we don't even know and probably wouldn't even like if we got to know them.

It was a typical punk rock song. Everyone clapped when their set was over.

Foghat, the popular boogie band from England who would, in time, grace the airwaves with "Slow Ride," was supposed to play next. But they cancelled. We already knew this because there was a big sign at the entrance of the concert that read: FOGHAT CANCELLED.

Everyone was intently watching the stage in hopes of seeing one of the The Guess Who getting ready to play. We were happy because we didn't have to sit through another opening act. The excitement was short-lived, though. The promoters had found a band to fill the spot for the errant British boogie-meisters, Foghat. Of course, it had to be the weed guy and his progressive rock band of so many different names.

"Hello out there!" the weed guy said. "I guess we're called Foghat Cancelled tonight. We were going to be The Ice Bowl Highlights. But now we're Foghat Cancelled because that's what it said on the sign outside. The sign outside is always right."

"Rock 'n' roll!" someone yelled.

"Yeah. Boogie!" someone else yelled.

The weed guy looked into the audience. "We'll save that for the encore."

Then the band played their "Dandelion Whine" song, the one about alien abductions and the competition in the quiz show. I thought the quiet part about the dandelion covered with poison and who had a friend who was a laboratory mouse with induced cancerous tumors was pretty good.

The guy next to me didn't think so. He just yelled, "Boogie!"

Someone else yelled, "Get off the stage! We want The Guess Who!"

The Clap played the opening chords to "American Woman."

Everyone applauded. People began to lift cigarette lighters in the air.

Then he stopped.

"Just kidding," he said.

Most of the people put their lighters away.

"We're running really late," the weed guy said. "Can you believe it? They will only let us play one more song."

People applauded. Enthusiastically.

"So," he said, "this one's about two dogs who get sent to the moon. One is called Otto and the other is called Fritzy."

"Go home! We don't want you here!" someone yelled. The crowd was getting hostile.

"These two dogs," the weed guy explained, "travel through the universe and claim whatever they find. They urinate on the place and then it's their property. Famous explorers did the same thing. Except they urinated and then they planted a flag."

"We don't like you," someone yelled. "Go away!"

"Now," the weed guy said to the heckler, "that could be the title of this song. That's what we are going to call it tonight."

"Yeah," The Clap said. "This is called 'Go away. We Don't Like You.'" He laughed.

"It was once called," the weed guy paused for effect. "It was at one time known as 'We Came In Peace for All Mankind.'"

"Let's face it," The Clap said. "We never went anywhere in peace. That's a load of crap."

The weed guy laughed. "You're right. But I really like that new title. And we can only play one more song. That's what the promoter said. So this is it. One more song. Yeah. This is it, and it's called 'Go Away. We Don't Like You.'"

They played the full thirty-minute version of the song. Indeed, they gave the people what they didn't want, and then some more that they *really* didn't want.

When they finished, two or three people clapped. There are always a few people who insist on being polite.

There might even have been one or two who liked the song. Of course, years from that night, wealthy Japanese progressive record collectors would pay big yen for the recording of the song, but we didn't anticipate the windfall of artistic expression performed in our presence at that moment. So we were just happy when they finished and left the stage.

The weed guy waved at us.

The Clap smiled.

Maybe they somehow had a glimpse into their future cultural value. Of course, it is possible they didn't really care about any of that sort of thing at all.

A guy with long hair who sat several seats from me was smoking a joint. I watched as he offered it to the girl next to him. I don't know if she was his girlfriend. She was young. The girl didn't say anything. She just took the joint. He was older and wore a T-shirt with the word REVOLUTION and the faces of The Beatles on it. That was their song and those were their faces, so he was probably a fan.

I could see the girl's face briefly illuminated by the tip of the joint. It burned like a really small ember of a much bigger fire whenever she inhaled. She was wearing mascara to cover up her young eyes.

Did those eyes want that pot?

We always want the forbidden fruit of Eden. Eve wanted the apple. Adam wanted Eve. Molly wanted Richard. Steve wanted to be Richard. Mr. U. wanted to make a record. The chubby carbon-copy kid wanted a bratwurst. I, of course, still wanted that Snickers candy bar instead of that Payday.

I heard a bottle shatter on the concrete floor of the arena. Brown booze, like the murderous slime from that movie *The Blob*, was suddenly everywhere in large puddles, moving slowly across the floor. The puddles weren't warm, like the blood of dead people in Vietnam. They were just cold.

The puddles had glass in them. It was glass from the bottle someone had smuggled past the security guard.

Somebody swore.

I figured it was the guy who had smuggled the booze and now had to watch the concert without his buzz.

Then the young girl with the old mascara eyes inhaled again. I saw the small ember glow in the darkness of the concert hall. I watched in the dim concert lights as two kids tried to lick the puddles of booze off the arena's filthy floor. They were like a twin perversion of Ponce de Leon sipping from the fountain of eternal youth.

I should have laughed because this was all part of The Revolution. This was the time and place I hoped to find.

But I couldn't laugh.

I just looked at the guy with the Beatles T-shirt and long hair. He was handing a joint to the poor guy who had lost his bottle of brandy. I was watching an ace salesman sell an old car with no guarantee to a kid who just wanted that car more than anything else in the whole world and didn't even care that there was no guarantee. I felt sad for that kid because he was forking over quite a bit for an oil slick promise and used car keys.

The weed guy was probably right. His Revolution was much better than all of this. Give the people what they don't want. Don't buy the debt. Don't swallow a Revolution. Don't inhale old age. Just leave the temple.

Maybe that's the best that any of us can do.

The Guess Who finally took the stage.

I still remember the look in Richard's eyes.

He watched in reverence as Burton Cummings and the

sweatshirt-clad Kurt "The Walrus" Winter walked onto the stage, which was raised rightfully high above us as we sat—mere mortals—in the third row folding chairs set up for this big rock 'n' roll event. For some reason, I noticed Kurt Winter, the star lead guitarist, had on some badly worn penny loafers.

The music was, of course, really loud, ear-numbing loud. The cigarette and marijuana smoke clouded the thick concert air, and the bright spotlights illuminated each band member. This diaphanous smoke formed halos of musical sainthood around these rock musicians who managed to rock the world a little bit that night.

They were our Guess Who.

We knew all the songs. This was all part of the show. This was our ritual. It was, in an odd way, a religious experience. They were like the gods. They were the gods we could never hope to be. So we worshipped them.

They were famous. They were gods, even though they sported badly worn penny loafers. They were cool. They were cool and they rocked the world a little bit. That was enough for me. That was enough for any of us in the crowd that night.

Yes, I do remember the color of Richard's eyes that night. He savored every syllable of every sound. If that moment was, indeed, all he really had, then he had quite a bit for which to give thanks. The Guess Who just played rock 'n' roll. I knew then that the world wanted to be rocked. That's all. The world doesn't care if you're sporting worn penny loafers. That's not important. It just wants to be rocked from time to time.

After the big concert, we went to the local Pizza Hut, our

ears still ringing from the music. The place was incredibly busy. Apparently, many of the other people from the concert had the same idea. Everyone wanted a pizza. Everyone always wants a pizza.

We hadn't waited that long for our order when, to Richard's absolute amazement, The Guess Who's Burton Cummings, the voice of "American Woman," and their guitarist, Kurt "The Walrus" Winter, wearing his sleeveless sweatshirt that said SOUND BY GARNET, walked through the door and stood by the counter.

Richard's jaw dropped to the Pizza Hut floor.

I nudged him with my elbow.

"Nobody knows who they are," I said. "Go introduce yourself. Get an autograph."

Richard was in shock. He tried to stand. Then he sat down. I had never seen him like this.

So I walked over to the band in his stead. I really had nothing to lose. I approached Burton Cummings, the lead singer, the man who had just sung his heart into ten thousand souls of the people at the show for more than three hours.

"Excuse me," I asked. "Aren't you Burton Cummings?"

Then one of the entourage people, maybe some sort of pharisaical bodyguard, shoved his hand against my chest.

"Look, kid," he said. "We've got a plane to catch. We're leaving in a minute. We're all really tired. Just let us get our pizza. Just leave us alone."

"I'm sorry," I said. "But one of your biggest fans is my friend. He's just sitting over there." I was desperate. "He'd love an autograph."

I looked at Burton Cummings. His eyes were cloudy

and distant, a victim of fame, perhaps. He heard what I had to say. His eyes suddenly changed. They were still really red-rimmed and tired, but they looked like the eyes of a fan. They looked like the eyes of a fan waiting for an autograph. They reminded me of The Monk's eyes when I returned his notebook.

I like to think, at that moment, he was a kid again. Maybe that was just wishful thinking. Suddenly this big rock star said to the entourage guy who still had his hand against my chest, "We're just waiting here. Get the pizza. It'll take a while."

He looked at me.

"Where's your friend?"

I pointed to Richard, whose eager face watched in total disbelief.

"Order one with pepperoni," Cummings said. "I'll wait over there." He motioned to Richard's table.

As we walked to meet Richard, I heard one of The Guess Who's entourage tell a waitress, "Don't you know who these people are? They're The Guess Who. They're a great rock band. They've had hit songs on the radio. We have a plane to catch. Can't you hurry things up? We want our pizzas."

The poor waitress, who was busy cleaning three tables, looked up in sad desperation and said, "I'm supposed to guess what?

"Look," she said, "I'm sorry. We're really busy. There was a big rock concert and everyone's here. I'd love to help. But we're really busy. Even God waits for his pizza tonight. There's nothing I can do about it. That's just the way it is."

I laughed. I thought she was being sarcastic. It was a funny thing to say. Then I noticed a small gold crucifix hung from a chain around her neck. She leaned to wipe a table and the cross almost struck an empty beer glass.

Maybe she meant what she said.

Maybe God really did have to wait for his pizza.

Maybe there really wasn't anything she could do about it. Who knows? Sometimes it's difficult to be certain about things like that. Maybe God really has to wait for his pizza. Maybe God was just like the rest of us.

Richard talked to Burton for quite a while. Not many people get to talk to their idol. Burton told Richard he had met Jim Morrison and they had driven around Los Angeles in Morrison's GTO. He said Jim Morrison loved the French poets. That surprised me, but I guess we're all fans, one way or another.

Kurt "The Walrus" Winter, the everyman guitarist, joined us for a moment. He asked me if I needed my glass. I didn't. That's what I told him. "The Walrus" then emptied the ice left in my glass on the Pizza Hut floor. I noticed a few of the ice cubes fell on his badly worn penny loafers. Then he filled my glass with beer.

"Thanks, kid," he said, and turned up the glass.

Shortly after this, Kurt was kicked out of the band for drinking too much.

The Guess Who was never really the same.

Magic comes as easily as it disappears.

Then everything is lost forever.

"The Walrus" died in 1997. He had problems with his liver for some time. I was really sad when I heard the news that he'd died. Even those people we deify—those people who rock the world a little bit, those people who wear the same clothes every day, those people whom we love—even those very same people have to deal with the darkness of their own demons in a hospital room.

Even God waited for his pizza that night.

HAMLET IN HELL?

A few days later, Lola, our ever-faithful setter, insisted on an early morning swim. She licked my face and barked repeatedly until I relented and walked her down to the Lake Michigan shore. There were stones and sunlight everywhere. The water was warm and gentle, so Lola paddled quite freely while I sat and watched from a sandy perch on the beach. I could hear the quiet groans of pleasure she made while she swam. From time to time, she would check back with me with a shower of setter shakes. I had seldom grown to love anything, but I loved that dog. Her tail wagged wildly as she ran back for another swim.

"Thanks, Lola," I called out. I was wet, but it was just impossible to be angry with that setter.

"Did she get you all wet?" I suddenly heard Steve's deep voice. Even when he spoke, I heard the music of Black Sabbath.

"Sure. But it's all right." I pointed to the lake. "Just look at her. She's gorgeous."

"Too bad she can't sing," he said.

I didn't reply.

"Then," he continued. "Then she could be in my band."

"What band?"

Steve smiled.

"My new band," he said.

Again, I didn't reply, although Steve could tell I wanted to ask about his new band. He grinned at me, waiting.

But I didn't have to ask him. I knew what he had in mind. I think the entire universe knew what he had in mind. It was that obvious. It had been planned so many times by so many other people who had never stood on the shore of a lake and watched a setter swim.

"Yeah, listen," he said slowly. "This is just between you and me." He looked at Lola as she swam in the lake. "Yeah, listen. This whole English Setter Dance thing is getting to be a problem, you know? Molly's gone. And this Geneva, she's all right. But she really gets on my nerves, you know? She just gets on my nerves. Richard writes all the songs. There isn't much room for us."

"For us?" I didn't follow his logic.

"You know. We wrote that song together. We can write more. You write your words. I'll write my music. Lennon and McCartney. Mick Jagger and Keith Richards. 'Satisfaction.' 'Get Off of My Cloud.' You know? We could do that. We could write songs. We could write really great songs.

"What do you think?"

I thought for a moment about my poem, "Branches Unseen," which had been used in "Our Tree Song" and its terrible Black Sabbath rip-off melody.

"So," I said. "You want more lyrics?"

"No," he said. "I want my own band. You and me. And we can talk Mr. U. into joining us as well. He'll play in any band that rocks. Our band will be a lot heavier than The Setter Dance. We'll be a lot better without Richard."

"So Richard's out?" I asked. "What about her?" I motioned to Lola who was still swimming in the lake.

"Hell," he laughed. "We'll get another dog. Maybe we'll get a basset." He laughed again. "Then we'll be The Basset Dance. That will be just as good."

"Who will sing?"

"Well," he was thoughtful. "Molly's out. She's gone. But she was a drag anyway because she never wanted to rock. So we'll keep Geneva for a while. She and Richard won't stay together very long. You know, Richard is always thinking about music. That's all he cares about. Then she'll get mad and join our band. She'll be all right. She gets on my nerves, but she'll be all right until we can get someone else. We'll keep looking. We'll find someone else. Then we'll get rid of her."

I picked up a stone and skipped it across the lake's surface.

"Why do you want me?" I asked. "I don't do much in the band."

"We're a team," he said. "You just write a few more poems about trees and pass them on to me. I'll worry about the music."

I didn't say a word, but I had visions of rewriting the entire Black Sabbath songbook. It wasn't a pleasant thought.

"Well," Steve said slowly, perhaps sensing my hesitation. "You just think about this. Keep this between you and me. We don't have to be second string, you know. We don't have to play his music. Just think about it." Then he walked away and disappeared into the woods.

"Just think about it."

It was about fifteen minutes later when Lola decided to

chase a few gulls. At first, she crept up to the birds, but as they scattered into the air, she began to run and bark. Her tail wagged in the sand of the excited beach air.

"She's really beautiful." I heard a voice say from behind me. It was Geneva, our stripper-singer.

She wasn't Molly.

"You don't mind if I have a swim? The water looks really warm." She began to pull her loose sweatshirt over her head. The sweatshirt had the word MICHIGAN printed on its front.

I didn't say no.

Then she dived into the lake.

"Come on," she yelled. "The water's warm! It's wonderful!"

"Damn!" I thought, eyeing her. What a time not to be able to swim.

"No!" I yelled and tried to cover up my fear of water. "I've already been in!"

"That's too bad!" She yelled back as she swam closer to the shore. Then Geneva stood, waist high in the warm water and brushed back her long blonde hair. "Well!" she said. "At least you could bring me my sweatshirt. I'm cold and I need to dry my hair."

I obliged. I just wish that I had thought enough to take my shoes off and roll up my pants.

"Thanks," she said. "But look at you. You're all wet. That's not good."

I watched as she pulled the sweatshirt over her head. "So," she said. "Do you want to join my band?"

I didn't know she had a band.

"Your band?"

"Yeah," she said. "I figure Molly is finally out. She's gone and that's good. She was always going to be out of the picture. She doesn't want to sing anymore. So I'll be the singer. I want to be the singer. I was born to be the singer. You understand. Richard said I could be the singer. Richard said so.

"I can make my English Setter Dance really big. I can do that. If you want to be famous, just stick with my band."

At that moment, I wanted to stick with her band. But at that moment, I was also standing waist deep in the lake having just handed her back her sweatshirt.

"You should learn to play bass.

"That Steve gets on my nerves." She shook her wet hair. "He's always trying to write songs. The guy has no talent. I can make him leave. Then you can play bass."

She walked slowly out of the water. Drops of water fell from her hair and gently rolled down the front of her sweatshirt.

I was envious of those drops of water.

"Sure," I said. "I can play bass."

"That's just great!" She pushed her hair back. I watched a few more lucky drops of water roll down her bare legs.

"Thanks for the swim," she added. "I just hope it wasn't too much trouble, you know. Getting my sweatshirt for me."

"Trouble?"

"Yes, I hope you didn't mind."

I didn't.

"Well, thanks," she said with a short laugh. Then I watched Geneva's wet legs as they ran from the beach back to the cabin.

Mr. U. wandered to the shore about ten minutes later. He was wearing a loose sweatshirt, too, but he didn't take it off. Lola liked Mr. U. When she saw him, she darted out of the water and ran setter circles around him. Then she barked. It was her game of tag. She just wanted to be chased.

"Chasing a setter in the morning," Mr. U. sang in one of his silly songs.

Lola barked again.

"Another song?" I asked.

"Yeah, but I'm not a songwriter. My songs are awful. That's all right, though, because I'm just the drummer. The drummer never gets to write the songs."

"Ringo wrote songs for The Beatles."

"They were just novelty songs. They weren't much better than mine."

I laughed and then asked, "Did you ever finish a real song?"

Mr U. smiled. "Drummers don't write the songs."

"No," I persisted. "Really. Did you ever write a good one?"

"Well," he kicked the sand with his shoe. "I am working on a song. Whenever I can get my hands on a piano, I'll work it all out."

"You play piano?"

"Sure. And guitar and flute and oboe. If you promise not to tell anyone, I might even admit to playing tuba in my high school marching band. If you tell anyone, I'll deny it. Remember, I'm just a drummer in a rock band."

"Your secret is safe. But what about your song?"

"It's about life. It's all about a big highway and we're all going too fast and we don't even know the construction people won't be able to keep ahead of us. Then we're going to all just drop right off the edge."

"What's the song called?"

"'Last Exit Ramp.' It's really heavy. It's too heavy for The Setter Dance to ever play. That's just as well, but the song's a warning. We all better get off the highway before it ends. We better take the last exit ramp because after that ramp, it's all over."

He paused, thoughtfully.

"Someday I'll finish it." He paused again. "And I know the name of my band. Not The Setter Dance. This will be the name of my own band."

"What's the name?" I asked.

"Rock 'n' Roll Heaven." he said. "And there's a period after Heaven. Once you get there, that's it. That's all there is."

"Are you certain about that?" I asked. "Maybe your band should be called Rock 'n' Roll Hell."

Mr. U. smiled. "No," he said. "I don't know very much, but I don't think there are any rock bands in Hell."

"Why not?" I asked.

He smiled again. "Rock music's just too cool."

I looked at Lola as she swam in the lake.

"What about setters?" I asked.

"Setters, dogs, they're just too kind to be there. Cats, maybe. Gerbils, for sure. Yeah. I can see gerbils in Hell. But not dogs. They're usually a lot smarter than we are." He shook his head. "No. There aren't any dogs in Hell. It just doesn't make sense."

"I once had a pet gerbil," I said.

"What was his name?"

HAMLET IN HELL?

"Hamlet."

Mr. U. laughed at that.

"I don't like to think of him in Hell."

"Well," Mister U. asked, "was he a good gerbil?"

I thought for moment.

"I guess so. He had really bad hair and he always seemed worried. But gerbils don't really get to do very much."

"Then how could he be in Hell? The universe doesn't work that way."

I was relieved. It was nice to think the universe didn't condemn good gerbils. It was nice to think my pets, my friends, and those people I love could rest in peace.

I was ready to follow Mr. U. back to the cabin when I noticed Lola had wandered off in search of shore birds again. So I called her name and walked a short distance until I saw her. Lola had found Richard, who was sitting by himself on a large rock. He was looking at the lake and he was tickling his setter. His guitar was nestled in his lap.

"Molly says thanks," Richard said.

"Molly?" I said. I had forgotten about Molly. I was still thinking about Geneva and her sweatshirt. I was still thinking about being unable to swim and the drops of water on Geneva's legs.

I suddenly felt ashamed.

So I looked away from Richard, who sat next to Lola on the beach.

"Well, she says thanks," he said again.

I looked at the moon, which weathered the morning sunrise to reveal its dim crescent curve. That moon knew the truth of this moment. The moon knew about Molly and the moon knew about Geneva. That moon knew about my shame. So I vowed if I ever were given the chance to hold the hand of someone I truly cared for, if I ever were given the chance to love someone, then I would hold her hand and look at the moon and never feel ashamed because I would not have anything about which to be ashamed.

I vowed to someday look at that very same moon and feel better than I felt at that moment.

Then I looked at Richard and noticed that he, too, was looking at the crescent moon.

"She says thanks?" I asked. "Thanks for what?"

"I really don't know," he said. "But she said I should say thanks for noticing her."

I thought about my talk with her after the last show with the band.

"She also says good-bye. She says that she just doesn't want to be in the band anymore."

"She's gone?"

"Yeah. She just left. I knew she wanted to go." He paused. "Now, Geneva will have to be the singer."

I looked at the sad moon. Then I looked at Richard. I saw the crescent shape reflecting in his eyes.

"She felt bad about you and Geneva," I said. "You've been spending so much time with her. She felt bad about that."

Richard smiled. I still saw the moon in his eyes.

"You sound like a man in love," he said. Then he corrected himself. "Actually, you sound like a man who's very much in love."

"In love?" I played innocent.

The moon looked hard at me again.

"Yeah. In love. You know, Geneva's all right. She's really different from Molly. She's different from most women."

"And you like that?'

"Not really." I looked in his eyes. They didn't want to talk about Geneva.

I tried again anyway.

"So you like her?"

He remained quiet. The moon just reflected much more deeply in his eyes.

So I asked about his songs instead.

I told him they were so different from most of what I heard. I told him I really liked his songs. I told him they were special to me. I felt naked.

"I wish," he said shyly, "I just wish I knew where they all came from."

"You're just talented."

"And that's a curse," he said. "It's a curse, you know. It's the bite from the apple. It's very bitter. Don't get me wrong. I love it. I love it a lot. But it's still really bitter. There's nothing I can do about that. Maybe being talented is just a matter of listening to the spirits out there."

He looked at the lake, following the reflection in the water up to the moon.

"Sometimes I think creativity is nothing more than the spirits finding someone stupid enough to listen to them. Maybe that's what creativity really is. Maybe it's just a certain kind of stupidity."

I felt uneasy with his confession, like a reluctant priest. And I didn't enjoy it.

"Did Molly say anything else?" I asked.

"Well," he said, "she said I should give you a kiss."

He laughed.

"Sorry, but you'll have to take a rain check on that one."

"Did she say anything else?"

He smiled. "You like her, don't you?"

Of course I liked her. I liked her a lot. But I chose not to answer.

The moon glared at me.

I remained silent.

"You keep that kiss," Richard said, finally. "You keep that rain check."

"I will."

And I meant it. I really did.

"Did you ever want to be with someone?" I asked.

"I'm with Geneva," he replied.

I sensed a lack of sincerity.

"No," I said, "did you ever know someone and think about her all the time. And words just stumbled out of your mouth every time you tried to talk to her?"

"Well, you've heard the song."

"Which one?" I asked.

"'Hold Me Tight On This Rock 'n' Roll Night.' It's about wishing I could tell a girl exactly how I felt about her.

"Writing songs is really great, but it's a curse, too. I can say anything in a song. It's almost too easy. But I can't tell a woman what I really feel. I guess that's all part of some deal with the devil. To write these songs, you have to sell your soul."

He smiled.

"That's the bet, and it's the only hand you ever get to hold."

I had to ask, "What was her name?"

"The devil?"

"No." I really wanted him to be serious. "What was the name of the girl you wrote that song for? Who was she?"

"It was a long time ago. I guess her name was Becky." He gave me a sly look. "Her name was Becky Leibniz."

"Did she ever know that you wrote that song about her?"

"Of course not. That's the deal. I wrote it all in that song. But I could never bring myself to say anything to her. I suppose after a while she just figured that I didn't care. And then one day there was just too much distance between us. Distance is an awful thing, especially when it's not a matter of miles or even just a few feet. This distance was all about lost moments and missed chances that never come again.

"I should have said something. But I didn't because I couldn't figure out a way. Then there we just distance between us.

"It's all a bit like the universe," he added. "There was just too much space."

I suddenly felt really bad for him. I told him I was sorry. That's all I could say.

"That's all right," he said. Lola jumped onto his lap. "At least I have my dog. And you have your rain check. You hold onto that. It's a good thing to have."

I knew that. I planned to keep it for a long time. It was the most important thing I ever owned.

"May I give you a little advice?" Richard asked.

"Sure." I expected wise words from my sage.

"Next time you walk in the water, it's all right to roll up your pants. Gods get to walk on water. We humans just get wet. You look like you just had an accident."

I laughed. "I'm usually not that stupid…"

"To be that stupid." He finished my sentence. "I know. I wrote the song. Believe me, I know all about being stupid."

Richard paused again, shaking his head sadly.

"But you need to keep that rain check. You need to collect that kiss."

"Thanks for the advice."

"Sometime in the future," he said slowly. "Sometime you go ahead and ask Molly if she remembers my Becky."

"She's the girl you wrote about in that song." I was eager to know more. "So Molly knows Becky?"

"Yeah. Ask Molly if she remembers Becky. She was a person we both knew a long time ago."

"Sure. I can do that."

"Oh. Don't do it right now. Not now. It's not important. Don't say anything right now. You've got your kiss to collect. That's important now. You have time for everything else.

"There's always time."

I smiled and thought about my rain check. Sure. I had time.

I looked at Richard.

I was certain we both had time to kill.

THE LOST CONTINENT OF IMAGINATION

The universe is always in motion.

Things always change.

Molly was gone. Geneva was our new sexy singer. No one really noticed the change except for a few fans who still waited for their "Stupid Song" and hooted and whistled when Geneva danced on stage sporting a really short skirt, really high heels, and all sorts of glitter.

Lola noticed, though. She didn't like it at all when Geneva tried to dance with her during her song. Lola sensed the difference the very first night. We were no longer just a little folk-rock band. Now there were so many more screams and lights and violence waiting in the wings of our performance.

Lola somehow knew her little dance just wasn't the same (or even wanted) in our show with Molly gone.

Richard played a new song that first night. He called it "The Lost Continent of the Imagination." I truly wish songs like that one could have been recorded. Richard's songs like "Onward, Christian Canines," "Thanks, Mrs. Clearwater," and "Lost Continent," are all gone now. They are all gone to wherever songs like that go. I would like to think they might end up in Crazy Carl's shop with the copies of the Foghat Cancelled album.

But I doubt it.

I would like to think they travel around and are the secret source of other songs for other bands.

But I doubt it.

I would like to think the songs are invisible and just out of reach because we can't see them, or touch them, or listen to them, even in our dreams.

But I doubt it.

Coincidentally, Richard's song about his "Lost Continent" was once called "I Doubt It." It was about Atlantis, that great mythical city lost forever at the bottom of the ocean. It was real, but now it's gone.

Richard's song was about the imagination being real like anything else that could be touched or seen or heard. The song was sad. In it, Richard lamented that we had all lost the way—the bridge—to the imagination. It was all gone, like Atlantis, and now we only talk about the imagination like we talk about the passenger pigeon, and the dodo bird, or the owner's manual to Stonehenge.

It was a sad song and, as I remember, because these songs were never recorded, the very last verse was about all the children who ever played at being pirates, giving up their treasure maps and coming to terms with the cold hard fact that Captain Kidd's buried gold was just too deep and too distant for their small shovels. For all these children knew or cared, the buried treasure—like the sunken city of Atlantis, like the secrets of the imagination—didn't exist anymore.

As I said, it was a really sad song.

The fans didn't pay much attention to the new song. We had worked up a medley of Steve's favorite, "Smoke On The Water," which could last for six or seven minutes, then Richard's song, Steve's fans' favorite, "I'm Not That Stupid To Be That Stupid." Then we would follow up with our dog's dance number, "Lola." That's all they wanted to hear.

The whole thing could last up to twenty minutes.

It always brought Steve's fans to their feet as they laughed and yelled about how great it was to be so stupid and loud. Of course, when we added Geneva and her tight skirt into the mix, it all became a lot more volatile. She sold excitement to the crowd, and she liked all the aggression with its pushing and sweating and screaming, as long as all the attention was focused on her. She was a natural at what she did so well.

I really think, in fairness to her, that she was sick and tired of all the lonely men with their dollar bills; she was sick and tired of all the lonely men who had long ago divorced themselves from the bedrooms of reality; she was sick and tired of all the lonely men who simply liked to watch her up on her stripper stage. On stage with us, she had those lonely men as they once were: loud, proud, drunk, and possibly not even certain any more where that place called Vietnam was in the world.

In a couple of years, the younger brothers of these louts would sing Bruce Springsteen's "Born In The USA," point a victory finger in the victory air, and confuse what happened in Southeast Asia with their own version of inebriated celebration.

During the first show with Geneva, one of our fans

became all worked up while we were playing "The Stupid Song," when Richard sang about fighting for the right of any pretty girl to pose for *Playboy* Magazine.

The guy started to yell at Geneva.

"Pose for me! Take it off!" he screamed.

Then he focused an imaginary camera at her while she sang. Geneva, standing right above the guy on the stage, shoved her high-heeled foot forward, and in the flash of the strobe light, rested her heel on the guy's shoulder. Then she kicked her foot hard. I even felt the kick, and I was standing at the back of the stage.

The idiotic drunken fan fell backward and knocked down two of his buddies who spilled their drinks on the dance floor. But the Not-So-Prince-Charming had grabbed our Cinderella's high-heeled slipper before he fell. I watched as he proclaimed, with Geneva's shoe raised high above his head, a fairy tale football victory chant for men everywhere. The guy even tried to scoop some of the booze from the puddle on the floor and drink from his high-heeled trophy.

His friends wanted to drink from the shoe, too.

I suppose it was all in good fun, but by the looks of the ugly mob who shook the guy and patted the Not-So-Prince-Charming on the back, their watches must certainly have marked the sad passing of the midnight hour; and yet I think, in retrospect, at that moment, mice and pumpkins would have been preferable to the rabble who grappled for the promise of a sip from their sacred slipper.

Our singer, now sans shoe, never missed a beat, and suddenly shouted to those fans something "about their flashbulbs popping." Of course, there were then multitudinous imaginary camera shutter clicks from the front row,

THE ENGLISH SETTER DANCE

pretend photographers vying for Geneva's attention.

Lola, bless her, refused to do anything that night. I don't know whether she was scared or whether she just didn't want to dance among all that commotion.

It was just as well. Geneva had the spotlight.

The word "cute," which was the best Lola could ever hope to be, just didn't describe any aspect of The English Setter Dance anymore.

It was really hard to believe how many fans appeared for our next show. This time they came with real cameras to snap their flashes at us during the highlight of the night, Richard's "Stupid Song."

Sure enough, when we played the first chords to the song, the guys all pushed forward to be the one on the receiving end of Geneva's high-heeled kick. Some bands, like The Who, were expected to slam their equipment to smithereens. Jimi Hendrix lit his guitar on fire. Genesis had strange costumes and weird stories. Ian Anderson of Jethro Tull stood on one leg and played the flute. Our little band now had a lead stripper-singer who was expected to kick a fan and have her shoe stolen as a souvenir.

I was there and watched it all. I have to admit, with the flashes popping in our faces all the time and the myriad of greedy hands reaching for Geneva's foot, the whole thing was getting dangerously out of control.

After a while, even that wasn't enough for them.

I remember the fourth or fifth show when the kick had already been delivered and the high-heeled shoe had disappeared into the crowd. The hands still grabbed blindly forward, reaching out for Geneva. It was like playing in a pit of slithering snakes.

The hands all wanted her other shoe, and each hand seemed to have a mind of its own.

They were all suddenly just there, without arms, or bodies, or faces. All the hands just wanted the other shoe.

Geneva noticed it, too, and yelled, "Come and get it!" into the microphone. No one could muster the courage to mount the stage, though. The hands slithered back, away from the lights. So Geneva taunted those reticent fingers, fingers coiling in the shadows of pregnant ambition.

"Come and get it!" she yelled again.

"Come on!" she taunted. "Come on and dance with me!"

No one answered her offer.

So she laughed and said, "Then I'll dance with the dog."

Poor Lola! She wanted nothing to do with any of this. She had infinitely more sense.

Geneva grabbed her front paws and tried to get her to stand on her hind feet. Frightened, Lola pulled away from the flashes and ran to the back of the stage, where she usually waited for her song. All of our fans, still a little embarrassed by their failure to produce a dancer for the stage, found Lola's fear and desperation crudely hilarious.

They clapped, and they hooted; they pounded their fists on the stage for more.

Good sense did not prevail that night.

As a result, Richard wanted to do the next show, which would turn out to be our very last real performance, without Lola. We had a big band meeting about this. Of course, Steve loved the fame and fortune, even if it was a little out of control. Geneva wanted the dog to be in her act.

Richard was not interested.

He and Geneva were never really friends, so when

things fell apart between them, there was nothing left at all. They were lead and gold with no common magic. Love, I suppose, requires an alchemist stone, and the rock onto which our music was fused just wasn't strong enough.

We had become a bit of a business with bookings and expectations and better money than we had ever seen when Molly had been in the band. So Richard ultimately relented, and I think Steve saw an opportunity to grab whatever power it was that he wanted to grab from the band; and why he wanted it, believe me, God only knew.

I certainly didn't understand any of it.

We were, however, locked into our image that included an ironically stupid song that few understood, a dancing dog who no longer felt like strutting her stuff, and a lead stripper-singer who predictably relished strutting all she ever had to strut. She just danced and sang on stage in front of our ever-growing legion of fans who really didn't care about our band. They all just wanted to be stupid and maybe grab a souvenir shoe.

Our last show was a mess, an oddball scary mess.

It started out all right. We played a couple of Who songs, although Richard's rendition of "I'm Free" obviously took on an irony all of its own. He still sang "No Sugar Tonight" and "Share the Land" by The Guess Who. He still played "Onward, Christian Canines."

Geneva sang a few of her own favorites by The Beatles that we had worked into the act. She sang "Paperback Writer" and "Come Together" and, in all fairness to her, a really potent rendition of Lennon's ode to Yoko, "I Want You."

Then Mr. U. and Steve started to pound the introduction to our trilogy. Steve and Geneva sang, "Smoke On The

Water," and the crowd began pushing and shouting for "I'm Not That Stupid To Be That Stupid."

Eventually, the outstretched hands fought for the feel of Geneva's foot. They begged to be on the receiving end of her kick.

And after the kick, of course, her high-heeled shoe was grabbed, and then to the victor went the spoils, such as they were. Flashes from all the cameras were popping in our eyes, and Geneva—lit in the strobe light frenzy of our fans' photography—offered an open dance floor on the stage.

"Come on!" she taunted. "Dance with me! Come on! Dance with me!"

Again, no one dared to take her up on her offer. No one had the guts to dance with her. No one had the guts to jump on stage.

So she said, "All right! I'll dance with that dog!

"At least she's not a coward!"

That was enough. It was more than enough, actually. That was too much more than enough.

The very next second our number one fan, the guy who told us that he really liked our "Stupid Song" because it confirmed for him that it was all right to beat his wife and smoke whenever he wanted, suddenly popped up on stage. He popped up just like another exploding flashbulb.

It was that sudden, just like a flashbulb.

He screamed. It was a sound unlike anything I had ever heard. It wasn't any word at all. It was just a sound, a hideous sound, the sound a dirty word makes as it is carved into a toilet wall.

Then he ripped off his shirt to show us all kinds of tattoos. There were all sorts of them, but the only one I could make out was the black swastika. Richard saw it, too. I know he saw it because he suddenly stopped. He just stopped playing his guitar in the middle of the song.

Then everything else stopped.

Let there be silence.

It was a dead thick silence, like the moment before the beginning of the universe. There was no music in that moment. Music didn't exist, just like that moment from Father Pontiac's letter, when Jerry Evans bled all over Mother Earth in Vietnam and Cpl. Greg understood that, without music, life just isn't worth the price of admission, especially when your friend had to die in a place so far from home, in a foreign land so distant from the warm childhood cocoons that are filled with games of war and free from the reality of the bloody glare in the dark retina of a swastika's worshipper.

So Richard, in complete silence, put his guitar on the floor and walked to the back of the stage. He took Lola's leash and simply walked out of the bar with her.

Steve launched into a heavy, thudding bass pattern. The guy with the cigarette and swastika tattoo picked up Richard's guitar and started to "play." The instrument wailed loud, earsplitting noises.

I had seen enough. I walked away from the stage.

As I left, I looked back, just like Lot's wife.

I wasn't turned to salt.

I wasn't that lucky.

As I glanced back, the beautiful music of Richard's band, our English Setter Dance, had been transformed by the guy with the tattoo, who had been joined on Mr. U.'s vacant drum stool by another fan who pounded away at those drums without the mercy of meter, or the awareness that others were attempting to play alongside him on stage that very moment.

He just hit everything really hard.

I felt a stone in my chest, and I then knew the greatest song—the most enduring piece of rock music I'd ever heard—had a flip side, a B-side, which might not be so wonderful.

I knew then that rock music was just like the human heart. Sure, there is great beauty, but there is also an awful lot of noise. And sometimes, when you're in the midst of all the excitement, it's not that easy to tell the two apart.

Music can, indeed, be the sound of The Revolution, and it can shake the walls of the city, and it can leave Jericho naked. Sometimes, though, The Revolution is nothing more than a guy in a Beatles T-shirt passing around drugs to score with a young girl who is hopelessly trying to cover up her youth, a youth that still clings, defiantly—just like the thick, dark mascara around her eyes.

It's always been that way.

Richard knew it all along.

That's why he was the first to leave the temple.

I followed.

The seas parted for me, too.

As I looked back toward the stage, the tattooed fan with Richard's guitar stepped to the microphone and chanted in a charcoaled voice:

Hitler was given a bad rap,
By idiots with lots of money!
I know that he butchered a lot of Jews,

THE ENGLISH SETTER DANCE

But I think that's really funny!
I'm not that stupid to be that stupid!

While he screamed this refrain over and over amid the roar of his horrid guitar and all the feedback of sound, I clearly knew the difference between the artful music of the heart—that elusive magic worth the sum total of a lifetime—and the obscenity of ignorance and hatred that is often willful and often a source of evil pleasure, the flip side of beauty, the stuff best left in Pandora's Box.

I watched Geneva, still in love with being the center of her own universe, mimic the tattooed guy's words, while scanning the audience for someone to kick. That's all she ever wanted: just someone to kick.

Unfortunately, just like our fans would never allow themselves to understand the irony of Richard's intent, and Jerry Evans' blood could never be poured back into his body, the door to Pandora's plague can never be closed. Swastika tattoos are too dark and deep to ever be rendered harmless and wiped spotlessly clean, even by those of us who have never felt the tattooer's needle.

I watched our number one fan sanctify the knife-edge of brutality without even a glimmer of ironic humor. Without any allowance for even the darkest chuckle of self-criticism, the whisper of our own foolishness, there was very little to be said of the value of the human race.

Irony is God's gift. It's here to make us laugh at ourselves. It's a great gift, even though it's a sad gift. Give the people what they don't want. That weed guy sang a song about aliens who had an economy based on the irony standard. Well, that night, those aliens would have passed us by. They would have left us alone in our ocean blue and cloud-covered world.

God. I felt so alone that night. I never want to feel that way again.

I wanted to be needed. I wanted aliens to need the irony of our world. I wanted to be held by someone. Pride didn't matter.

I just didn't want to feel ashamed anymore.

I couldn't even feel contempt for the whole thing. I only felt the total disinterest that others in the universe must feel toward creatures like us, who at that moment knew no irony; we who at that moment knew no humor, we who had no purpose, except maybe to a few hard-nosed parasites or sundry space entities still traversing the old slave-trading routes of the universe.

The hot air was thick; and it dripped, like royal blood must have dripped from Macbeth's hands after Duncan was dead.

I turned away in silence. I heard the crowd laugh at the spectacle. I heard them applaud, though I really doubt if anyone could say Amen to the night's ceremony. At least a few people managed to say that after Father Pontiac's drunken sermon.

No one in the bar that night could even think of the word Amen. I know that I couldn't think of a word to say.

And I certainly didn't hear anyone else trying to pray.

BETTER THINGS

The band gathered a few days later for a big meeting.

Richard spoke first.

"We have to start all over. We have to get back to the way we were when we began." He dictated his terms to the rest of the group.

"That last show was disgusting. It wasn't even music." He looked at Steve. Their eyes met. I knew this was hard for Richard to do because he and Steve had been friends for so long.

"But we're finally getting somewhere," Geneva spoke up. "People are coming to the show. After that last one, more will want to see me sing and dance." Geneva was attempting to wield some power. The truth was that she was concerned about her position in the band. She was only the singer because Molly left and Richard had dated her a few times.

That was over now.

She and Richard barely spoke to each other anymore.

"That Nazi stuff wasn't really my fault," Steve said.

Richard eyed him contemptuously. "You kept playing."

"And you left. We still had to play. We had to play until they closed the bar. That was the deal."

BETTER THINGS

Mr. U., who had been quietly ruminating in a corner, finally spoke up.

"Let's just play some music. Everything will be all right if we just keep playing music."

Richard shook his head.

"I'm not going to play that song any more. I hate watching those idiots get wild. Look, that song was never meant to be any good. It was just a stupid idea. Either those people will never get the joke or they don't want to get the joke. It really doesn't matter. I won't play it."

Steve looked worried.

"So we leave out the best song? That's why they come to see us."

"That's right. We leave it out." Richard's words seemed to lay down the gauntlet to Steve. Something in the atmosphere of the room changed at that moment. Not only had Richard drawn a line in the sand, but I also knew Steve had stepped across that line.

Everything changes. You can never go back.

This was one of those moments. Words could never be erased. Steps could never be retraced.

"That's it then," Steve said slowly.

"That's right," Richard said. "We leave it out. I won't play it. I won't play it ever again. Maybe they'll get tired of us and just go away."

"Then where will we be?" Steve raised his voice. "Do you want to hear the people puking to your songs again?"

Geneva suddenly chimed in again.

"So what do I get to say about all of this? I'm the singer. I'll sing whatever songs I want to sing."

"You can shut up!" Steve shouted at her. "This is between Richard and me! You don't matter."

He looked at Richard.

"Look, the band's doing a lot better. So you don't like the swastikas and Nazi stuff. Big deal! I don't like most of the songs you write. And then you finally write something people like, something that makes them pay to see us. And you didn't even think the song was any good. I'm the one who figured out we should play it. We even made that record. And now you don't like it. You won't even play it!"

"That's right. I won't play it. And you can't play it without me."

Steve knew he was right.

"What about 'Smoke On The Water?' We have to play that. It's my song. I sing that one."

"I don't care about that song. I just don't want the crowd to be so crazy. We have to play music like we played before all those people began to show up. It's just crazy. Those people just want to get drunk and be stupid. So let's get rid of all that stuff."

"What about 'Lola?' " Steve asked.

"Sure. She can stay. It would be great to see her dance again. But now she's scared all the time."

"No," Steve said. "I was talking about the song."

"Yeah," Richard thought for a moment. "We can keep that. I'll just have to figure something to replace the 'Stupid Song' in the middle. We can still do the other two."

Steve looked thoughtful.

"A new song?" There was a skeptical tone in his voice. "It had better be good."

BETTER THINGS

He paused.

"No," he said. "It had better be great."

"Great?" Richard laughed.

"That's right." Steve had a mean look in his eyes. "If it isn't great, I won't play it."

Richard laughed again, but there was no sign of humor in his face.

"Trust me," he said. "I'll come up with something. Just trust me.

"Things have to get better."

THE PRICE OF AN APPLE

Richard, as always, came through for the band.

His new song was called "The Beginning of the End of the Beginning." Or, to be quite truthful, it might have been "The End of the Beginning of the End." After all these years, it's difficult to be certain. Maybe it really doesn't matter all that much. Maybe we have yet to understand all that stuff like beginnings and endings and birth and mortality.

Mark Lesitermier, if you recall, was deemed a math genius in my high school because he could figure the price of apples in some high school mathematical word problem. The answer was sixty-seven cents. Of course, it was the correct answer. That's the sort of thing we know. We can count that, and we can sell that, so it's correct.

Richard's brand new song was about everything else. It was about everything we can't count and everything we can't sell.

I really don't think anyone in the band understood the new song. Richard just told us it wasn't about the price of an apple. So we took him at his word.

Richard always said things like that. That's what I remember the most about him. He liked being elusive, all the while putting the truth right in front of us.

THE PRICE OF AN APPLE

Richard always smiled when he was elusive.

In truth, his new "End and Beginning" song was all about friendship. It was really quite long, like an old Bob Dylan song with too many verses. It was an Old English style ballad about two very young English soldiers who fought in The French and Indian War and became close friends when one soldier saved the life of the other soldier. After the battle—and chronicled in the fourth verse of the song—the two new friends huddled together and laughed because a saved life, especially amid the countless other unsaved lives already rotting on the smoky battlefield, was really quite a miracle.

But Richard's new song was also about the passage of years and the changing tides of political oceans. In twenty years' time, with the French defeated on the Plains of Abraham, the English fought their new wave of an enemy, the upstart American colonies, with the very same two soldiers, now sadly divided: the one who was saved on the side of Revolutionary Americans and the other still loyal to George III and the crown of England.

In the hurry and blood of battle, the man who had been saved twenty years before suddenly found his friend midst the smoke and fear and noise.

Their eyes met for a moment.

And in another moment, the Revolutionary American soldier jabbed his bayonet into the chest of the Englishman, whose mouth opened as his eyes quietly fell back into his soul and blood spurted from his chest.

The very last verse of Richard's new song wasn't about the second battle and the death of the loyalist soldier, though. Richard recreated the hug between those two young men, who were happy and alive after a battle with the French. They didn't care about the future. They didn't know about The Declaration of Independence, or Bunker Hill, or a Delaware River crossing, or that moment in which their eyes would meet in the smoke and fear and noise of war.

Richard simply ended the song with the miracle of the moment when one man saved the life of another man.

This final verse, the last Richard ever wrote, didn't make the bayonet blade any less sharp; it didn't make the gash in the Englishman's chest any less painful; it didn't make the blood spurting from the man's wound any less red; but I was really glad the last song Richard wrote ended with two friends hugging each other.

Maybe this was the way Richard really wanted the world to be. This was the song he wrote to replace "I'm Not That Stupid To Be That Stupid." Was it as great as Steve wanted it to be? It's really hard to say. Richard only performed it once for our fans, so it's hard to say.

And I really don't know.

Looking back after all these years, I think Richard just might have been wrong.

The song was, in reality, all about the price to be paid.

When I set out hitchhiking to find The Revolution, I was sick of school and its mathematical word problems because they asked for equations about the price of apples. I didn't think that had anything to do with life.

I was wrong.

Life is always about that price.

Of course, there is no real mathematical answer. The only real answer is the amount any one of us is willing to pay to leave the temple. That's what The Revolution is really all about. It's not about cars, or long hair, or strippers, or Beatles T-shirts, or drugs, or broken bottles of booze, or tickets to concerts, or young girls with old mascara eyes.

It's not even about being right when everybody else is wrong.

The Revolution is just the price any one person is willing to pay to get out of the temple. It's the price paid for allowing a few weeds to blossom in the pristine grass of our existence. It's the price paid for opening the door to the gerbil cage. It's the price paid for Hamlet's choice. It's the price served on the silver platter. It's the price for saying Amen with a modicum of conviction.

Mrs. Clearwater paid the price when she lost her job. In time, Richard would be asked to pay a lot more than that.

We called Rock 'n' Roll Randy and told him that Richard wanted to play The Sled Shed again, just like we did a long time ago. In true Rock 'n' Roll Randy fashion, he mumbled something about "The Beatles, Horslips, The Kinks, and The Village Green Preservation Society."

That's how I like to remember Randy. He always had a rock band in his head. He was so innocent and he was always singing songs. I wish he still did that.

Back then, when he was the Randy we knew, he did anything we asked him to do, so he arranged the whole show for us. We told him the band wanted to go back and start again. I certainly wanted this. I just hoped no one would throw up when we played our music this time.

On Thursday, a few days before we played The Shed, I talked Mr. U. into driving to Molly's house, where she was living with her mother since she left the group. As always, she looked really great. She told us she was planning to go to college. She'd had enough of taking a chance at fame and fortune in our little band.

She really wanted to know how Lola was doing, though.

She was worried about our setter.

"You have to come to our show Saturday night," I said hopefully.

"Why? I'm over all of that."

"You have to come to see us. The band's been crazy since you've been gone."

"I hear you've been playing a lot."

"Sure," I said. "But it's been crazy with Geneva. Richard walked off the stage in the middle of a song. It's that bad. And Steve and Geneva kept playing. Then these idiots from the crowd played on stage. It was just noise. Mr. U. and I left, too."

"It wasn't rock music," Mr. U. said. "I couldn't play anymore."

Molly looked at both of us.

"I don't want to sing in a band," she said. "I don't want to do that now."

"You don't have to sing. Just be there. Maybe that will help us."

I pleaded with her.

"Richard wants us to play like we did when you were the singer. He won't play that 'Stupid Song' in the set. Steve's really mad. There's some new song. We need you Molly. At least be there. That might be enough to save us."

"That song about being stupid wasn't that bad," she said.

"Sure," Mr. U. laughed. "At first it was fine. Then all those idiots started to show up and dance on stage and grab at us.

THE PRICE OF AN APPLE

We're a band. We play music. That's not rock 'n' roll. Come on, Molly. At least come and see us. We need you there."

"Richard needs you," I added.

Molly looked at me.

I suddenly felt ashamed.

"How about you?" she asked.

"I want you to come," I confessed. "I really want you to come."

"When is it?"

"Saturday, at The Shed. The show starts at eight. It'll be just like when we started.

"I promise."

She smiled. "Sure. I'll be there. It'll be just like old times."

"Maybe you could even sing one song."

"Yeah, maybe."

On Saturday, the day of the show, I was really nervous. Not because of my playing in the band. I still didn't contribute very much. It was just that this show meant so much to all of us. We couldn't keep going the other way. It was too wild and stupid. I had fallen in love with all the music we played. I had fallen in love with Richard's odd songs, and I had fallen in love with Lola, our dancing setter. I just wanted our band to continue. I wanted to play music forever.

That night, I kept glancing into the crowd, hoping to see our Molly sitting somewhere in the audience. Richard was there, and Steve, and, of course, Mr. U., but Geneva was nowhere to be found. Her absence spoke volumes. If she couldn't sing and dance and be the star as much as she wanted, she just wasn't going to show up.

Some people are like that.

When it became obvious she was a no-show, Richard simply laughed. It was a sad laugh. He took the blame.

Steve was angry.

Mr. U. just wanted to start playing his rock 'n' roll music.

So the band played on.

We began with several of Richard's songs. He wanted to take control of the music. I know we played "Onward, Christian Canines" and "Thanks, Mrs. Clearwater." Those were both favorites of mine. It's just too bad they are only recorded in my memory.

Then we played "I'm Free" and "Won't Get Fooled Again." Richard always loved The Who's songs. That night he sang the words to those songs like they were lava erupting in the midst of our music. And, as expected, all of our fans were crowded and pressed into the area around the stage, their eyes scanning for signs of Geneva.

Meanwhile, I searched the audience in hope of seeing Molly's face somewhere amid the smoke in the bar. Finally, I saw her hair. She turned toward the stage and smiled at me. I suddenly thought about the moon. I waved at her.

Then the fans that were pushing themselves toward the front of the stage started to yell. "Where's the girl?" they screamed. "We want the girl!" One even pleaded, "Kick me! Kick me! Kick me!"

Richard answered their cries.

"Look," he said. "Look. This is about the music tonight. Just let us play our music. The music should be enough. Nobody's going to get kicked. It's just music. That's all we're doing tonight. Just the music. We don't have a girl singer anymore. It's just us now."

"Where's the girl?" they yelled. "That girl's gotta kick me!"

Mr. U. spoke from the back of the stage. He didn't even bother to sing the words like he usually did.

"There isn't a girl in the band anymore."

Then the first fan, the guy with the tattoos, began to scream.

"Then you have to kick me! I gotta get kicked! Kick me! Kick me! Kick me!"

My God! I felt like kicking the guy. Hell, Mohandas Gandhi would have felt the urge to give the guy a swift boot in the head.

Then I heard Molly's voice over the din. She was singing "The Battle of Evermore," the duet she and Richard sang so beautifully. Her voice hovered, beautifully angelic above the screams.

She was back.

I felt the comfort of a familiar friend.

We really needed that. Richard paused for just a moment, smiled, and then strummed the necessary chord. The English Setter Dance was alive again, and for an excited heartbeat of four simple songs, we were in Heaven. Steve, Mr. U., Richard, and my Molly transcended the smoky noise of all our idiot fans to make really beautiful music together. In addition to "The Weight," we played my favorite, "The Story in Your Eyes," and, finally, a wonderful version of Richard's ode to nature, "My Happiest Days."

Those songs sounded so good to me after not hearing them for so long.

There are moments in life that make all the bad times and mediocre times almost worthwhile. We humans can come together in a communion of sorts because it's in our nature. We have the gift to care about each other and work for a greater purpose than ourselves, a purpose with a higher calling than a single voice, a purpose with a heart that's damn big and generous.

I've seen it happen a few times in my life, and I know that I saw it alive and well for the life span of those four little songs.

It's an amazing thing, really. It's probably too amazing to last very long.

I watched sadly as the moment disappeared. It was barely there, just like Mrs. Clearwater's wink. It was gone too soon because it meant too much in a world that's never willing to give us much for very long.

Richard once told me Mrs. Clearwater stopped working in the department store shortly after her boss had yelled at her for opening so many albums for him. Her replacement was a young guy with long hair. Richard said he was all right, but he never opened albums for anyone anymore. Richard said the long-haired guy never got into trouble with the boss and he never winked at anyone.

Smart people claim the purpose for the horrid darkness in life is to allow the bright times to be more vivid, more luminous. That might be true, but no sunrise, no glorious burst of starlight, no refulgent moment of my life left to be lived will ever enlighten this black hole in my memory or impart sufficient meaning to what I witnessed back then.

Richard's smile widened, satisfied, as he finished the last chord of "My Happiest Days."

But the fans had heard enough. They wanted to dance. No. They wanted to kick and push and scream. They wanted their song. They wanted their "Stupid Song."

THE PRICE OF AN APPLE

Steve hit the bass notes for "Smoke On The Water." They cheered. They knew this was the prelude, the start of their ritual, the start of their cruel game.

Steve did his best to shout his way through "Smoke." Then—and to this day I do not know if it was meant as a joke or just a mean thing to do to his friend Richard—Steve suddenly played the opening bass notes, not to Richard's new song, but to the song we had vowed never to play again, "I'm Not That Stupid To Be That Stupid."

The crowd squeezed against the front of the stage. They pushed and shoved.

Then they went crazy.

Richard and Mr. U., stunned by the unexpected bass line introduction, just played like zombies who were caught up in Steve's ill-conceived idea. Richard glared at Steve. I saw our bass player mouth his message in one word: "Gotcha."

So Richard stopped. He simply refused to sing the words. He said he would never sing that song again, and he meant what he had said. Of course, the fans could not have cared less for Richard or his vow. Nothing was sacred to them. They saw their blink of an opportunity and, in terrible unison, seized it and shouted out the words they all knew by heart:

> Sure, kids all over the world are starving,
> But they're really easy to ignore,
> Because I've got pizza in the freezer,
> And five cold beers in the refrigerator door!
> I'm not that stupid to be that stupid!

They put their arms around each other while they swayed

to their own singing. Some even opened lighters and flicked their flames, which danced about the heads of the mob like a pestiferous profanation of a Pentecost.

It made me sick.

Richard's mouth dropped open, and he closed his eyes. We both understood that ignorance, whether real or just a mean joke, is a beast that plagues us all. There is no escape. There is only a matter of degree of this ignorance. The best any of us could ever do is to put one small human finger in one of the myriad holes of the dam, knowing that there is just too much water, too much ignorance, on the other side. Richard knew he didn't have enough songs and he didn't have enough fingers to plug all the vacant holes in the bar that night. But songs and fingers were all he had, so Richard did the only thing he could do: he began to sing his brand new song about two friends who hugged each other.

He started singing "The Beginning of the End of the Beginning" against the wave of the crowd-sung "Stupid Song."

The fans began to chant, "Stupid! Stupid! Stupid!"

They wanted their song.

They wanted only their song.

They wanted their song and they jumped on stage to get it.

They wanted their song so badly that they grabbed Molly and started to yell, "Come on and dance!"

Poor Molly just froze there, unable to move.

They wanted their song and they shoved her aside.

They wanted their song and they marched to the rear of the stage and grabbed our cowering dog Lola by the scruff of her neck.

Three of them lifted her three or four feet off the ground. Lola squirmed in intense pain. She was suffocating.

The tattooed guy yelled, "Then I'll dance with the dog!" He pulled on Lola's neck. Her body and tail swayed like a hangman's noose, while she coughed and spit and choked.

"Dance, dog!" they all yelled.

Then they laughed.

We stood there, helpless, except for Richard.

He ripped his guitar from his shoulder and threw it at the dark stage. It spun through the smoky dense air and smashed against the floor, where it broke into pieces. The sound was demonic noise, the terrible sound of music breaking apart. Whole notes became half of what they should be. Then they were quarter notes, then eighth notes, and, finally, one solitary sixteenth note was left to fall off the musical scale into nothing, nothing at all. A million stars seemed to fall, like dying embers of some big fire from the night sky around my eyes.

Through the fog of it all, I heard Richard shout one last thing: "Leave my damn dog alone!"

They did.

There were three of them.

Each one gave Richard a hard shove against his chest. Three shoves, and I just stood there. Three shoves, and I didn't do a thing. Three shoves, and I stood frozen in fear.

I only watched, horrified, as they grabbed at Richard.

Later, in court, they would testify to the word "push" but, no, that was not what I saw at all. I saw the three of them lift and throw Richard toward the back of the stage. Richard stumbled, attempting to regain his balance. He did this horrible and awkward dance as he tried to recover his stability.

Then he looked at me. I must have been just a blur for a hurried second in time. I saw his face, and then his body arched forward, creating a huge silhouette on the wall. His left eye, which was the only one visible to me, suddenly winked.

It was very quick, but I swear I saw his eye wink at me.

Whether he winked to send some last moment message, or he was wincing in anticipation of great pain, I will never know; and that's a shame because, even after all these years, I really would like to know what he meant by that wink, what he was trying to say to me.

Then I saw Steve, Richard's friend, do something that still haunts my memory. Steve will always deny the truth, but I know what I saw, and what I saw is the truth.

I saw Steve step aside and let Richard fall off the stage head first in a half-somersault, into the brick wall behind the stage. His head and neck split apart like a piece of fruit; maybe like an apple and maybe not, but it made an awful sound.

I suppose it was just one more sound among a night of horrible sounds, but it was a sound I will never forget as long as I live.

Richard fell limp to the floor of the bar.

He lay still. His blood was very red, and it formed a halo of mortality around his head.

That halo of blood became larger as we watched.

Only Lola, his dog, had the decency to jump from our elevated position on the stage to tend to her human, her friend. She stood next to him — her paws immersed in

Richard's pulsing blood, licking his face in an odd reversal of that Bruce Springsteen song, "Reason to Believe."

I know Lola truly believed if she just licked that face long enough, her human, her friend, would rise up and be all right.

That's all she wanted.

Such was the heart of that beautiful dog.

Steve just stood there, silent.

I remember his eyes blinked really quickly up and down, up and down.

Molly screamed.

I should have yelled or cried, but my mind was just consumed in prayer, a prayer asking God how this was all possible because the war in Vietnam, the war of our generation, was over and kids no longer had to die.

Sure, Jerry Evans was dead. I understood that. But we were not going to be drafted. This was 1974. We weren't going to die. We were all Isaac. That's what I thought.

I didn't scream or yell or cry.

I just thought about that.

I just thought about being Isaac.

I scanned the audience for an answer. My eyes met the riveting stare of that Vietnam vet, the one I had seen at our very first show, the night of Richard's joke about Communists in Hawaii; he was the one with an arm missing, the one who still wore his army jacket, the one with the arm of his jacket pinned to its shoulder.

His eyes met mine. His eyes saw that my face was now his face. And I knew then that all the jokes told for the rest of my life would never be quite so funny, and that my laughter would only be a soft shadow of what it was before this blood-blackened night.

Rock 'n' roll Randy cried, and I remember his tears were big and watery tears, tears that made popping sounds as each one struck the stage.

There were many tears and there were many big popping sounds, like the distant disturbance of an ever-approaching war. Those tears were the only sounds I heard from him. He had no rock 'n' roll words left to say.

Our Richard died that night.

There wasn't a struggle for life. He no longer struggled against ignorance. There was just no more music to be made.

Our band ceased to exist.

All that remained was a black hole in a black night.

Outside, Molly and I stood shivering and shaking, holding each other for the first time. I don't know why we did that. It wasn't all about love. I think we wanted protection, although we both knew that was too much to ask.

Richard was right. I remembered his words. I whispered to Molly, "This moment is all we've got, so praise all gods and thanks a lot."

She tightened her grip and held me closer, but she didn't say a word.

We held each other for a long time. It was the only way to express how we felt. It was all we had. We both understood that. I certainly felt that way as my hand clenched the cloth of her dress so tightly that my fingers began to ache like they were frozen and all alone on a cold autumn night.

But I didn't let go.

I didn't let go.

THE PRICE OF AN APPLE

If the pains in my fingers were part of this whole thing called life, then so be it. If the terrible, ungodly ache spread to my arms and into my chest and to my heart, then so be it. And if these salty tears are not enough to extinguish the fires of that infernal night, even as they rage in my memory after all these years, then so be it.

So be it.

So be it.

THANKS, RICHARD

I sat on the quiet sandy shore of Lake Michigan, the very lake of Richard's rest. His ashes were scattered in its waves. It wasn't eternity, but it was so big and so beautiful that it provided an illusory glimpse into all other worlds.

There are so many ghosts in the lake and, when I listened, all of these ghosts seemed to sing songs.

I hoped Richard was happy.

I thought about him as I sat on that beach, and I just hoped he found some sort of rest.

I still had the old guitar I played with the band. I tried to remember all of his songs, the words and chords and melodies. I could play a reasonable version of "Onward, Christian Canines." And I had written my very first real song called, "Thanks, Richard." Thanks for the music. Thanks for the stories. Thanks for The Revolution.

I thanked Richard for so many things.

His only reply was the soothing sound of the waves lapping slowly against the lake's shore.

It was as beautiful an answer as I could ever expect to hear.

I heard a woman's voice in the somewhere nearby. When I found her, I could see that she was walking her dogs, two dachshunds, on the lakeshore's trail. She wasn't having much luck because the lead dog kept pulling on its leash. With his barely bridled effort, the hearty dachshund propelled the woman down the park path.

"No! Otto!" the woman commanded. "Otto! You're a bad boy! You get back right now!"

The dachshund continued to strain at its leash, until he suddenly stopped, lifted his little dachshund leg, and went to the bathroom.

"Otto!" she scolded. "Now I suppose you think that you own this place. What am I going to do with you?"

She looked down at the other dog as he walked heel-perfect at her side.

"Otto! Why can't you be more like Fritzy? You're a good boy, Fritzy. You know you are my boy. You're a good dog."

The second dog, Fritzy, glanced at his owner, grinned, and then, in a burst of dachshund speed, sprinted to keep pace with the other dog.

"Otto!" the woman screamed. "See what you've done!" She shook her head. "Fritzy! You get back here! Right now! Why must you always do what Otto does?"

Both dogs pulled the woman down the trail and away from my view. I could, for some time, still hear her yelling. "Otto! Fritz! Get back here! Otto! Otto! You get away from that tree! Oh no! Do you have to do that here?"

It was good to know some songs are much more real than we ever thought they could be. The weed guy would be proud.

Lola was swimming in the lake. She always liked the water. Perhaps she felt closer to Richard. She was mine now. I had to learn to play her song. I watched her dance.

Molly was on the beach, too. I watched as she walked toward me, picking up bits and pieces of driftwood and shells. She noticed a tiny fish flopping and gasping in the sand of the shore after it had been swept by the movement of a wave, beyond its control, to the very edge of the beach, where other dried fish had already met their parched death.

Molly gently picked up the flopping fish and cradled it back to the water of the lake. She was close enough so that I could hear her words.

"It's too soon to die," she told the tiny fish. "Go and give fish life another chance. Just because all the others are dead doesn't mean that you have to die."

I played a bit of "I'm Free" by The Who.

It seemed like the appropriate thing to do.

I hoped the tiny fish liked the song as it swam away from the temple.

I looked at Molly. Then I looked at my beautiful Lola, who was still swimming in the lake. I realized that every so often it is possible to fall in love at first sight. Perhaps even the Fates need to wink. It was as close as I've ever come to an actual miracle but, all things considered, one miracle in your life is a truly great thing.

If it's all just a matter of luck, then I'm just lucky.

Molly sat down beside me and we both watched Lola swim. There were drops of water and bits of sand on her legs.

"Do you think she knows that he's out there?" Molly asked.

"Dogs are really sensitive," I replied. "So yeah. She knows. She knows everything. And she seems so happy in the lake. So she knows he's there."

THANKS, RICHARD

"What do you think is out there?" Molly asked.

"Fish," I said immediately. "Big ones and little ones; and shipwrecks, I suppose, ghosts of sailors, dreams of getting back home. A lake can be really dark at night."

"No," Molly's voice was quiet and beautiful. "No, I was talking about, you know, what's out there, where Richard is now. Do you think he's playing music? Do you think he gets to listen to a new album by Jethro Tull?"

She paused.

"Do you think Mrs. Clearwater gets to play records for him?"

I really wanted to tell her my hunch, that there was no real rebirth. There is no glorious resurrection. There is no ultimate redemption.

I wanted to tell her all we humans have are the sad destructive fires of our own mistakes and the ashes of our own mortality.

That's about it. That's all there is. But there is goodness—even a simple greatness—in picking through those ashes in your hand, and in the full realization of the ephemeral nature of life, creating something new from the fallen, something new from the old, something new from the devastation of our own stupidity.

I wanted to say that, but instead I just said, "Richard's playing music somewhere. I know he's playing music because I listen, and I hear him playing one of his songs. And I always think he's playing his song just for you, Molly."

I looked at the water and the bits of sand on her legs.

"I think he knows how much you liked his music. He knows the truth about everything now."

She smiled.

"Then he's not playing the song for Molly," she said. "He's playing it for Becky."

"Becky?" I asked. "What do you mean?"

"Molly," she said with a forced smile. "Molly Maloney. That's just a name I made up a long time ago when I was just a little girl because I wanted to be famous. The other kids at school said my real name wasn't good enough to be famous. They made fun of my name. So I made up Molly. I made up Molly so she could be a famous singer. I didn't have a fancy name, so I made one up.

"When everyone made fun of me because of my name, I knew that I had a different name and it was a famous name. So I felt better."

I was surprised. "You look like a Molly to me," I said.

"Well, I'm not a Molly."

"What's your not-so-famous name?" I asked.

"Becky," she said. "Becky Nothing."

"Becky Nothing? Boy. You weren't kidding. That really isn't a famous name."

She grinned.

"No, I just said that because it doesn't matter anymore. That's what the other kids called me. Kids can be cruel sometimes. Maybe they said that because I told them I wanted to be famous."

"So, Becky Nothing," I said. "What's the real something?"

"Becky Leibniz," she replied. "My father even gave me a middle name that made everything worse. Mona. Imagine that for my middle name. Mona. That was my great-grandmother's name."

I thought about all of this for a moment. Molly. Becky. Mona.

THANKS, RICHARD

It didn't really matter. It honestly didn't matter anymore.

"How about Molly Mona," I suggested. "Then you could be half famous. Being half famous is about as much as we really need."

"I'd settle for a quarter." She thought for a moment. "I'd settle for a lot less than that, actually. Things like that don't matter anymore."

She was right.

The English Setter Dance mattered, but not because we became rich and famous. To this day, very few people even know or care that our little band ever existed.

But the band did matter.

The English Setter Dance mattered because we had tried to make something beautiful in a world where beauty doesn't always get the chance to exist for more than a wink of an eye, and that's not a very long time.

Then Molly said, "Who knows? Maybe someday someone will write a book all about this, all about our band. Then we can all be a quarter famous."

We both laughed.

They were the first real laughs we'd shared since Richard's death. They weren't much, but they felt good. They were all we had left.

"You know," she said, "I always wanted to thank you."

"For what?"

"You wrote that song about me."

"You mean 'Branches Unseen?' The one I wrote with Steve?"

"Yes, I thought it was so beautiful. You took the time. You noticed. You noticed me enough to write those words about me. That mattered. No one ever did that before. No one ever cared enough to write a song about me.

"You were the first one, so that was special."

I thought about Richard's confession on the beach. He had written about his Becky, too. He, too, wanted to hold her tight on that rock 'n' roll night. Now she would never know there had been another song written about her. She would never know about his love. She would never know about the sad distance between them.

I didn't know what to say.

I didn't know anything about the truth any more.

The truth is a lot like The Revolution. They're both really hard to figure out.

I remembered Father Pontiac's words. I had asked him to speak at Richard's funeral. I was afraid he might be drunk again, but he wasn't drunk at all. Father Pontiac had just said he had watched Richard play his music. He confessed he had heard him play in a strip club.

We all laughed a little bit at that.

He said it was a shame, from what he had been told, that there was no music playing when Richard died. I told him that. He said there should always be music playing when a young person dies. He said that without music, the death of a young person is just too awful.

And, he said, this was awful. It was just too awful.

Then he asked us why young people had to die in wars. He asked why young people had to die in anger. He asked why young people had to die because of stupidity. He said young people should have fun. He said they should have their lives in front of them. Father Pontiac said he didn't know the answer to any of this. He confessed he had no answer, and he said adults should have answers.

There was genuine sadness in his voice.

He was sorry about not having answers.

Father Pontiac then sighed and took a breath and said something I still deeply recall from the memory of that distant day. I still have a copy of his eulogy for Richard he so kindly gave to me. It's carefully folded in a box next to the paper with my handwritten lyrics for "Branches Unseen." I have read his final words for Richard so many times they have become worn and faded just from being read with so much love and thought and appreciation. That's what words are for: to become worn from years of tender consideration.

Father Pontiac told us all the love which is hidden, love which is unrequited, love which is sung in song yet not confessed in the midnight caresses lighted only by the candle flame of mutual passion, love unfulfilled and left on the bloody battle fields of foreign wars, love locked in the ego-infested trenches of our own selfish wars of the heart, love which never speaks the metaphors found within its own pentameter, these are the true tragedies of our own short lives.

"Perhaps," he said, "young beautiful people never really push the rocks that seal their tombs.

"Perhaps," he added, "we should stop asking them to push those rocks."

Then Father Pontiac said it was all just an idea and that music was strong stuff. He said Richard's music was strong stuff. He said Richard's music was really strong stuff.

Thanks, Father Pontiac.

Thanks for saying that.

I also remember the small group of people who came

together for Richard's funeral fell completely silent during these final words. Words are meant for silence. And, oddly enough, silence is meant for words.

Mr. U. was there.

Buzz Hogey was there.

My enemy, Junior Weston, was in the crowd, but at that moment I just didn't care about a football catch.

The weed guy was there. He wasn't dressed in his weed costume.

The three girls from the graduation party were there. They started to sing the same song they sang at that party. It was a song from Pink Floyd's *Dark Side of the Moon*. Everyone slowly joined in their chorus.

Rock 'n' Roll Randy was there. He didn't sing at all. I don't believe he could accept the fact that those like Richard, who are touched by the gods to play beautiful music, could ever die.

But we do. We all die. The good, the bad, and those—like most of us—who are somewhere in between.

We all live and we all die.

Poor Rock 'n' Roll Randy.

This was not his world. This would never be his world. He would never understand Richard's song. He could never praise all the gods, and he could never say thanks a lot.

But I could.

I could say that, but I couldn't tell Molly about Richard's song, the song he wrote about his bashful love. I could only hold her, arm-in-arm, on the shore of that vast expanse in front of both of us.

I looked up at the moon as I held Molly. I wasn't ashamed. I held her close. I wasn't ashamed for anything I had ever done.

Of course, I wasn't proud, either. I knew too much to ever be proud again. But at least I wasn't ashamed.

I called Lola from the lake. She shook off water long enough to make all three of us wet and sandy. Then our Lola scrambled up the inclined beach slope that led to a path amongst the trees, a path that led us home.

Lola turned back and barked at us several times because we were so slow, but the two of us took our time anyway, holding hands, as we walked in the difficult, deep beach sand up to that path in the woods.

It was the path that led us to the rest of our lives — lives uncertain, but lives certain to always be together.

A FEW QUESTIONS
AND A FEW ANSWERS:

The English Setter Dance has religious undertones.
Is this intentional?
Well, it is an interpretation of The New Testament—sort of.
Richard Lamm, I suppose, is a Christ figure. Peter tells us
Richard's story. Of course, it's all set in the rock music scene
of 1974. That's a mighty long way from Steinbeck's Dust Bowl
America with Jim Casey and the Joad family. But Christ did
tell Peter "upon this rock I will build my church." Perhaps
he was talking about rock music. But then again—perhaps
not. And there is Greek mythology in the book, too. I have
a friend who is a practicing Greek Mythologist—so I suppose that's a bit of religion—the door to Pandora's Box is
opened and all the trouble starts. Of course, Hope is eventually left behind. By the way, Mrs. Clearwater is John the
Baptist. There's quite a bit more. Steve is, of course, Judas.
And The Temple is whatever needs to be left behind—but
that's your business.

The Vietnam War is an important part of the book?
It's a metaphor. It's another war. Wars just seem to show up.
The "Isaac story" in the Bible is pretty clear. What's there
not to get? Let's stop killing kids. I don't know. Maybe you
had to be there.

Why are dogs important?
I don't really know. I write about them a lot. Perhaps they
are the last bit of Eden available to us. A puppy belly exists
to be tickled. I suppose that a puppy belly is a lot like rock
'n' roll. The Beatles probably managed to tickle us. Or they
gave us a belly to tickle. Who knows? John Lennon is dead.
He would know. But as I said, he's dead.

Does God really have to wait for his pizza tonight?
Odd question — I just ordered a pizza. How's that for irony?
But maybe that's what makes God so special. We like to
put our own human attributes on God. We all want to be
powerful and rich. Humans want that sort of thing. We
simply project our own desires onto some sort of deity.
Heaven help us! Let's get beyond our humanity. Or, I don't
know. Let's understand our humanity. Whatever, the pizza
delivery man is here, and I have to pay the poor guy and
give him a tip.

So Molly and Peter are together?
Life is uncertain. That's the only certainty. But I think Pip
and Estella are somehow still together. Stories are funny
that way. Words only chase the horizon. I know that they
want to be together. Molly is getting old. Peter is even older.
Molly makes the effort to save worms stranded on the

neighborhood roads during her daily walks. She puts them back on a grassy area so they can do whatever worms need to do. That's a nice thing. The last time I saw them, they were weeding their garden. And they weren't arguing.

And what about Rock 'n' Roll Randy?
Well, he never was able to give me a copy of The English Setter Dance's single. But he was really happy to provide the photo of the group for the cover. He told me, "The Kinks, man. 'Picture Book.' Yeah, 'Picture Book' of people with each other to prove they loved each other—a long time ago." That was pretty great. What a guy!